W9-BED-205

Reese whirled Madelyn around to face him.

"Don't walk away when I'm talking to you."

"Well, excuse me, Your Majesty!"

"If you want to go to town, I'll take you," he said in an iron-hard voice. "Otherwise, you keep your little butt here on the ranch, and don't you ever, *ever* leave the house without letting me know where you are."

"Let me tell you a few things, and you'd better listen. I'm your wife, not your prisoner. I won't ask your permission to buy groceries, and I won't be kept locked up here like some criminal. If you take the keys to the car or do something to it so it won't run, then I'll walk wherever I want to go, and you can bet the farm on that."

Very deliberately Madelyn bent down and lifted the bucket of water, then upended it over him. The water splashed on his head and shoulders and ran down his torso, to finally end up pooling around Reese's boots.

"If that isn't enough to cool you off, I can get another one," she offered in an icily polite tone.

Also available from MIRA Books and
LINDA HOWARD

ALMOST FOREVER
THE CUTTING EDGE

Coming soon

AGAINST THE RULES
MIDNIGHT RAINBOW

LINDA HOWARD

DUNCAN'S BRIDE

MIRA BOOKS

If you purchased this book without a cover you should be aware
that this book is stolen property. It was reported as "unsold and
destroyed" to the publisher, and neither the author nor the
publisher has received any payment for this "stripped book."

MIRA

ISBN 1-55166-051-2

DUNCAN'S BRIDE

Copyright © 1990 by Linda Howington.

All rights reserved. Except for use in any review, the reproduction or
utilization of this work in whole or in part in any form by any electronic,
mechanical or other means, now known or hereafter invented, including
xerography, photocopying and recording, or in any information storage or
retrieval system, is forbidden without the written permission of the publisher,
MIRA Books, 225 Duncan Mill Road, Don Mills, Ontario, Canada M3B 3K9.

All characters in this book have no existence outside the imagination of the
author and have no relation whatsoever to anyone bearing the same name
or names. They are not even distantly inspired by any individual known or
unknown to the author, and all incidents are pure invention.

MIRA and the star colophon are trademarks of MIRA Books.

Printed in U.S.A.

To Marilyn Elrod, my good friend,
who also taught me how to play
Shanghai and Spite & Malice

ACKNOWLEGMENTS

I had several sources for the trivia and obscure facts that I used in this book. I would like to acknowledge *Myth Information* by J. Allen Varasdi, Ballantine Books, New York, 1989; *First for Women* magazine, January 1990 issue; and *Instant Facts* from the World Book Desk Reference Set, Chicago, 1983 edition.

1

It was time he looked for a wife, but this time around he wasn't looking for "love" as part of the bargain. He was older and infinitely wiser, and he knew that "love" wasn't necessary, or even desirable.

Reese Duncan had made a fool of himself once and nearly lost everything. It wouldn't happen again. This time he'd choose a wife with his brain instead of the contents of his jeans, and he'd pick a woman who would be content to live on an isolated ranch, who was willing to work hard and be a good mother to their kids, one who cared more about family than fashion. He'd fallen for a pretty face once, but good looks wasn't on his list of requirements now. He was a normal man with a healthy sex drive; that would be enough to get the kids he wanted. He didn't want passion. Passion had led him into the worst mistake of his life. Now he wanted a reliable, common sense woman.

The problem was, he didn't have time to find her. He worked twelve to sixteen hours a day, trying to keep his head above water. It had taken him seven years, but it looked like this year would put him in the black, finally. He had lost half his land, a loss that ate at his soul every day of his life, but there was no way in hell he would lose what remained. He had lost most of his cattle; the huge herds were gone, and he worked

like a slave taking care of the remaining heads of beef.
The ranch hands were gone, too; he hadn't been able
to afford their wages. He hadn't bought a new pair of
jeans in three years. The barns and house hadn't been
painted in eight.

But April, his ex-wife, had her outstanding debts,
incurred before their marriage, paid. She had her
lump-sum settlement. She had her Manhattan apartment, her expensive wardrobe. What did it matter to
her that he'd had to beggar himself and sell his land,
his herds, wipe out his bank accounts, to give her the
half of his assets to which she felt "entitled"? After
all, hadn't she been married to him for two whole
years? Hadn't she lived through two hellish Montana
winters, entirely cut off from civilization? So what if
the ranch had been in his family for a hundred years;
two years of marriage "entitled" her to half of it, or
its equivalent in cold, hard cash. Of course, she had
been more than happy to settle for the cash. If he
didn't have that much, he could sell a little land. After all, he had oodles of it; he wouldn't miss a few
thousand acres. It helped that her father was a business magnate who had a lot of connections in Montana as well as the other western states, which
explained why the judge hadn't been swayed by
Reese's arguments that the amount April was demanding would bankrupt him.

That was another mistake he wouldn't make. The
woman he married this time would have to sign a
prenuptial agreement that would protect the ranch in
case of divorce. He wouldn't risk so much as one
square foot of the dirt of his children's heritage, or the
money it would take to run it. No woman was going

to take him to the cleaners again; she might leave, but she wouldn't leave with anything of his.

Given the way he felt, he would have been just as happy to remain single for the rest of his life if there hadn't been the question of children. He wanted kids. He wanted to teach them to love the land as he had been taught, to leave that land to them, to pass on the legacy that had been passed on to him. More than that, he wanted the life that children would bring to the empty old ranch house, the laughter and tears and anger, the pain of childish fears and the shouts of joy. He wanted heirs of his bone and blood. To have those children, he needed a wife.

A wife would be convenient, too. There was a lot to be said for available sex, especially since he didn't have the time to waste trying to find it. All he needed was a solid, steady, undemanding woman in his bed every night, and his hormones would take care of the rest of it.

But unmarried, marriageable women were scarce in that part of the country; they were all packing up and moving to the cities. Ranch life was hard, and they wanted some excitement in their lives, some luxuries. Reese didn't have the time, money or inclination to go courting, anyway. There was a more efficient way to find a woman than that.

He'd read a magazine article about how many farmers in the Midwest were advertising for wives, and he'd also seen a television program about men in Alaska who were doing the same. Part of him didn't like the idea of advertising, because he was naturally a private man and had become even more so after his disastrous marriage. On the other hand, he wouldn't

have to spend a lot of money just put a few ads in the
personal sections of some newspapers, and money
meant a lot to him these days. He wouldn't have to
meet the women who didn't appeal to him, wouldn't
have to waste time driving here and there, taking them
out, getting to know them. He didn't particularly want
to get to know them, not even the one he would eventually choose to be his wife. There was a hard layer of
ice encasing him, and he liked it that way. Vision was
much clearer when it was unclouded by emotion. The
impersonality of an ad appealed to that part of him,
even though the private part of him disliked the public nature of it.

But he'd decided that was the way to go, and Reese
Duncan didn't waste time once he'd made a decision.
He would put the ad in several of the larger newspapers in the West and Midwest. Drawing a pad of paper toward him to begin framing how he wanted the ad
to read, he wrote in bold, slashing strokes: WANTED:
A WIFE...

Madelyn Sanger Patterson sauntered back into the
office after lunch. You never got the sense that Madelyn had hurried over anything, her friend Christine
mused as Madelyn strolled toward her. Nor did you
ever think that Madelyn sweated. It was ninety-five
degrees outside, but no dampness or wrinkles marred
her perfect oyster-white dress, set off by the periwin-
kle silk scarf draped artfully over one shoulder. Madelyn was a clotheshorse; everything looked good on
her, but her own sense of style and color added a pa-
nache that stirred women to envy and men to lust.

"You're a disgusting person," Christine announced, leaning back in her chair to better appraise Madelyn's approach. "It's unhealthy not to sweat, unnatural not to wrinkle, and ungodly for your hair not to get mussed."

"I sweat," Madelyn said with idle amusement.

"When?"

"Every Tuesday and Thursday at 7:00 p.m."

"I don't believe it. You give your sweat glands an appointment?"

"No, I play racquetball."

Christine held up her fingers in the sign of the cross to ward off the mention of exercise, which in her opinion was the eighth deadly sin. "That doesn't count. Normal people sweat without exertion in weather like this. And do your clothes wrinkle? Does your hair ever hang in your face?"

"Of course."

"In front of witnesses?" Satisfied she had won that exchange, Christine looked pleased with herself.

Madelyn propped herself against the edge of Christine's desk and crossed her legs at the ankle. It was an angular, almost masculine pose that looked graceful when Madelyn did it. She tilted her head to study the newspaper Christine had been reading. "Anything interesting?"

Christine's mother always mailed her the Sunday edition of their newspaper from Omaha, so Christine could stay up-to-date on local news. "My best friend from high school is getting married. Her engagement announcement is here. A distant acquaintance has died, an old boyfriend has made his first million, the drought is driving feed prices sky-high. Usual stuff."

"Does she hold the old boyfriend against you?"

"Nah. She couldn't stand his guts when we were dating. He was a know-it-all."

"And it turns out he did know it all?"

"Evidently. It's disconcerting when things turn out to be exactly as they seemed."

"I know," Madelyn sympathized. "It's hard on your natural skepticism."

Christine folded the paper and handed it to Madelyn, who enjoyed newspapers from different cities. "There's a good article in here about relocating to a different part of the country for a job. I wish I'd read it before I left Omaha."

"You've been here two years. It's too late for culture shock."

"Homesickness is on a different timetable."

"But are you really? Or are you just in a blue mood because you broke up with the Wall Street Wonder last week and haven't found a replacement yet?"

Christine sighed dramatically. "I have a bad case of heartbent."

"What's a dent to a Sherman tank?"

"Bent, not dent!"

"Then shouldn't it be 'heartbend'?"

"That sounds like something you get from diving too deep, too fast."

"Surfacing."

"Whatever."

They grinned, content with the exchange, and Madelyn returned to her own office with the newspaper in hand. She and Christine honed their wits on each other with mutual enjoyment while still maintaining a totally amicable relationship. Madelyn had learned early that not everyone enjoyed that kind of conversation. Several teenage boyfriends had been, in various degrees, insulted, angered, or intimidated, which had promptly ended her fledgling relationships with them. Boys were too caught up in their hormonal urges and too wildly protective of their newfound masculinity to tolerate what they saw as the faintest slight to that masculinity, and unfortunately, Madelyn's lazy wit often seemed to offend. She sighed, thinking about it, because somehow it didn't seem that things were much different now.

She stared at her desk. It was disgustingly and disgracefully clear. She could either stay at the office for the rest of the day or go home, and it wouldn't make a bit of difference either way. Odds were, no one would even know she had left, unless she stopped on the way out and made a point of telling someone. That was how often her phone rang.

There were advantages to being the stepsister of the owner. Boredom, however, wasn't one of them. Being idle was excruciating for her. The time was swiftly approaching when she would have to kiss Robert's cheek, thank him for the thought, but politely decline to continue with this "job."

Maybe she should even consider moving away. The West Coast, maybe. Or Fiji. Robert didn't have any business concerns in Fiji. Yet.

She unfolded the newspaper and leaned back in her chair with her feet propped on top of the desk and her ankles crossed. The decision would wait; she had been working on the problem for some time now, so it would still be there when she finished reading the paper.

She loved out-of-town newspapers, especially the smaller ones, the weekly editions that were more folksy gossip-columns than anything else. The Omaha newspaper was too large for that kind of coziness, but it still had a midwestern flavor to remind her that there was, indeed, a life outside New York City. The city was so large and complex that those who lived in it tended to be absorbed by it. She was constantly looking for windows on other ways of life, not because she disliked New York, but because she was so curious about everything.

She skipped over World Affairs—they were the same in Omaha as in New York—read Midwestern and local news, learning how the drought was affecting farmers and ranchers but creating a booming business for the slaughterhouses, and who had married or was intending to. She read the sale ads, compared the price of real estate in Omaha to that in New York, and was, as always, amazed at the difference. She was skipping around through the want ads when an ad in the personals caught her attention.

"Wanted: a wife for able-bodied rancher. Must be of steady character, want children, and be able to work on ranch. Age 25 to 35 preferable."

Those interested should contact said able-bodied rancher at a box number in Billings, Montana.

Madelyn was instantly diverted, her imagination caught by the ad, though she wasn't certain if she should be amused or outraged. The man was practically advertising for a combination brood mare and ranch hand! On the other hand, he had been brutally honest about his expectations, which was oddly refreshing after some of the personal ads she'd seen in the New York newspapers and magazines. There had been none of that slick "Sensitive Aquarian needs a New-Age Nineties woman to explore the meaning of the universe with him" hypersell that told one nothing except that the writer had no concept of clarity in the written word.

What could be learned about the rancher from that ad, other than his honesty? His age could be anywhere from fifty on down, but since he wanted children she thought he would be younger—probably in his thirties or early forties. Also, that bit about children probably meant one could take the able-bodied part literally. If he wanted a wife of steady character, he probably wasn't a party animal, either. He sounded like a sober, hardworking rancher who wanted a wife but didn't have the time to look for one.

She had read an article several months ago about mail-order brides, and though she'd found it interesting, she had been put off by the impersonality of it all. It was evidently a big business, matching Oriental women with men in Western nations, but it wasn't limited to that; farmers and ranchers in the less-populated states had started advertising, simply because there were so few women in their areas. There was even an entire magazine devoted to it.

Really, this ad was the same in intent as the slick ads: someone was looking for companionship. The need was the same the world over, though it was often couched in more amusing or romantic terms.

And answering the ad was doing nothing more than agreeing to meet someone, like a blind date. It was a way of making contact. All relationships began with a first date, blind or otherwise.

She folded the paper and wished she had something to do other than ponder the issue of social advertising.

She could go upstairs and pound on Robert's desk, but that wouldn't accomplish anything. Robert didn't respond well to force; he wouldn't disturb the smooth running of his offices just to give her something to do. He had offered her the job as a means of giving her a focus in life after losing both her mother and grandmother within a short length of time, but both of them knew that the job had outlived its purpose. Only an incurable optimism had kept her at it this long, hoping it would turn into something legitimate. If she pounded on Robert's desk, he would lean back in his chair and smile at her with his wickedly amused eyes, though his mouth seldom actually joined his eyes in celebration, and say, "The ball's in your court, babe. Serve it or go home."

Yes, it was time to go on to something new. The shock of grief had led to inertia, and inertia was even harder to handle, otherwise she would have left over two years ago.

Wanted: a wife.

She picked up the newspaper and read the ad again.

Naw. She wasn't that desperate. Was she? She needed a new job, a change of scenery, not a husband.

On the other hand, she was twenty-eight, old enough to know that the swinging life wasn't for her. Nor was city living, really, though she had lived in cities most of her life. As a child in Richmond, she had dearly loved the weekends when she had visited her grandmother in the country. Though it had been only a rural house, not an actual farm, she had still reveled in the peace and quiet, and longed for it when her mother had remarried and they had moved to New York.

No, she wasn't desperate at all, but she was curious by nature and badly needed a diversion while she decided what sort of job she should look for, and where. It was like a first date. If it clicked, then it clicked. She had nothing against Montana, and wouldn't that be a wild tale to tell her grandchildren, that she'd been a mail-order bride? If, as was far more likely, nothing came of it, then no harm had been done. She felt far safer answering an ad from a Montana rancher than she would one from a freestyle urbanite.

Feeling a bit exhilarated from the daring of it, she quickly rolled a sheet of paper into her top-of-the-line electronic typewriter, wrote a reply to the ad, addressed an envelope, put a stamp on it and dropped it down the mail chute. As soon as the silver metal flap swallowed the envelope, she felt a peculiar, hollow feeling in her stomach, as though she had done something incredibly stupid. On the other hand, she had had this same feeling the first time she'd gotten behind the wheel of a car. And when she'd ridden one of the super rollercoasters. *And* when she'd gone to college, flown for the first time, and gone on her first date. This same feeling had accompanied almost every first in her life, but it had never been a forerunner of disaster. Instead she had thoroughly enjoyed all those firsts. Maybe that was a good sign.

On the other hand ... a mail-order bride? *Her?*

Then she shrugged. It was nothing to worry about. The odds were that she would never hear from this Montana rancher. After all, what could they have in common?

Reese Duncan frowned at the New York return address on the envelope as he slit it open and removed the single sheet of typewritten paper inside. What would anyone in New York know about life on a ranch? He was tempted to toss the letter into the trash; it would be a waste of his time to read it, just as this trip into Billings to pick up the mail had been a waste of time. Today there had been only this one response to his ad, and from New York, of all places.

But the overall response to the ad hadn't been exactly overwhelming, so he might as well read it. In fact, this was just the third answer he'd gotten. Guess there weren't too many women in the world anxious for life on a Montana ranch.

The letter was short, and remarkable in the information it *didn't* give. Her name was Madelyn S. Patterson. She was twenty-eight, had never been married, and was healthy, strong and willing to work. She hadn't sent a picture. She was the only one who hadn't.

She was younger than the other two women who had responded; they were both in their thirties. The schoolteacher was his age, and not bad to look at. The other woman was thirty-six, two years his senior, and had never worked at a paying job; she had remained at home to care for her invalid mother, who had recently died. She was plain, but not homely. Both of them would have far more realistic expectations of the vast, empty spaces and hard life on a ranch than this Madelyn S. Patterson.

On the other hand, she might be some small-town girl who had moved to the big city and found she didn't like it. She must have read his ad in a home-town newspaper that had been mailed to her, because he sure as hell hadn't wasted his money placing it in the *New York Times*. And he hadn't had so many re-sponses that he could afford to ignore one. He would make the same arrangements with her that he'd made with the others, if she were still interested when he wrote to her.

He tapped the folded letter against his thigh as he left the post office and walked to his pickup truck. This was taking up more time than he could truly af-ford. He wanted to have everything settled by July, and it was already the middle of May. Six weeks. He wanted to find a wife within the next six weeks.

Madelyn almost dropped her mail when she saw the Montana address on the plain white envelope. Only nine days had passed since she had answered the ad, so he must have replied almost by return mail. In those nine days she had convinced herself that he wouldn't answer at all.

She sat down at her small dining table and ripped open the envelope. There was only one sheet inside.

Miss Patterson,
My name is Reese Duncan. I'm thirty-four years old, divorced, no children. I own a ranch in cen-tral Montana.

If you're still interested, I can see you two weeks from Saturday. Let me know by return mail. I'll send you a bus ticket to Billings.

There was no closing salutation, only his signature, *G. R. Duncan*. What did the *G* stand for? His handwriting was heavy, angular and perfectly legible, and there were no misspellings.

Now she knew his name, age and that he was divorced. He hadn't been real before; he had been only an anonymous someone who had placed an ad for a wife. Now he was a person.

And a busy one, too, if he could only spare the time to see her on a Saturday over two weeks away! Maddelyn couldn't help smiling at the thought. He certainly didn't give the impression of being so desperate for a wife that he had been forced to advertise. Once again she had the distinct impression that he was simply too busy to look for one. He was divorced, the letter said, so perhaps he had lost his first wife precisely because he was so busy.

She tapped the letter with her fingernails, studying the handwriting. She was intrigued, and becoming more so. She wanted to meet this man.

Madelyn S. Patterson had answered promptly, which the other two hadn't; he had yet to hear from them. Reese opened her letter.

Mr. Duncan, I will arrive in Billings on the designated date. However, I can't allow you to pay for my travel expenses, as we are strangers and nothing may come of our meeting.

My flight arrives at 10:39 a.m. I trust that is convenient. Enclosed is a copy of my flight schedule. Please contact me if your plans change.

His eyebrows rose. Well, well. So she preferred to fly instead of taking the bus. A cynical smile twisted his mouth. Actually, so did he. He had even owned his own plane, but that had been B.A.: before April. His ex-wife had seen to it that it had been years since he'd been able to afford even an airline ticket, let alone his own plane.

Part of him appreciated the fact that Ms. Patterson was sparing him the expense, but his hard, proud core resented the fact that he wasn't able to afford to send her an airline ticket himself. Hell, come to that, even the bus ticket would have put him in a bind this week. Probably when she found out how broke he was, she'd leave so fast her feet would roll back the pavement. There was no way this woman would work out, but he might as well go through the motions to make certain. It wasn't as if applicants were beating down his door.

Madelyn invited Robert to dinner the Thursday before her Saturday flight to Montana, knowing that he would have a date on Friday night, and she wanted to talk to him alone.

He arrived promptly at eight and walked to her small liquor cabinet, where he poured himself a hefty Scotch and water. He lifted the glass to her, and as always his eyes smiled without his mouth joining in. Madelyn lifted her wineglass in return. "To an enigma," she said.

He arched his elegant dark brows. "Yourself?"

"Not me, I'm an open book."

"Written in an unknown language."

"And if your covers were *ever* opened, what language would be there?"

He shrugged, his eyes still smiling, but he couldn't refute the charge that he held himself off from people. Madelyn was closer to him than anyone; his father had married her mother when she was ten and he sixteen, which should have been too great an age difference for any real closeness, but Robert had unaccountably taken the time to make her feel welcome in her new home, to talk to her and listen in return. Together they had weathered first the death of his father, then, five years later, that of her mother; most stepsiblings probably would have drifted apart after that, but they hadn't, because they truly liked each other as friends as well as brother and sister.

Robert was a true enigma: elegant, handsome, almost frighteningly intelligent, but with a huge private core that no one was ever allowed to touch. Madelyn was unique in that she even knew that core existed. No one else had ever seen that much of him. In the years since he had inherited the Cannon Companies, he had reshaped the various enterprises and made them even larger and richer than before. An enormous amount of power rested in his lean hands, but not even the Cannon empire seemed to reach that private center of him. The inner man was a citadel, inviolate.

It was as if he kept himself leashed, his fires banked. Women flocked around him, of course, but he was particular in his bed partners and preferred monogamy to musical beds. When he chose a particular woman friend, they were usually together for at least a year, and he was entirely faithful to her for as long as the affair lasted. One of his ex-amours had gotten drunk and cried on Madelyn's shoulder at a party shortly after Robert had ended their affair, sobbing that she would never be able to love another man because how could anyone compare to Robert? The woman's drunken confession had, so far, been pathetically accurate; she had drifted into a couple of affairs, but both of them had been short-lived, and since then she had stopped dating entirely.

Now he was watching Madelyn with his amused eyes, and after a minute she answered her own question. "Your language would be an obscure one, dead, of course, and translated into a cipher of your own invention. To paraphrase Winston Churchill, you're an enigma inside a puzzle wrapped in a riddle, or some such complicated drivel."

He almost smiled; his lips twitched, and he dipped his head to acknowledge the accuracy of her assessment. He tasted the Scotch, savoring the smoky bite of it. "What's for dinner?"

"Conversation."

"A true case of eating our words."

"And spaghetti."

He gave the Scotch a pained look and set the glass down; he didn't think it would go well with pasta. Madelyn gave him an angelic look that deepened the amused expression in his eyes. "So what are we conversing about?"

"The fact that I'll be looking for a new job, at the very least," she said as she went into the kitchen. He followed her, and without hesitation began helping her carry the food to the table.

"So it's time, is it?" he asked shrewdly. "What made you decide?"

She shrugged. "Several things. Basically, as you said, it's time."

"You said, 'at the very least.' And at the most?"

Trust Robert to see the implication of every little word. She smiled as she poured wine into their glasses. "I'm flying to Montana this Saturday."

His eyes flickered just a little, signalling his intense interest. "What's in Montana?"

"Not what. Who."

"Who, then?"

"A man named Reese Duncan. There's a possibility of matrimony."

There were times when a look from Robert's pale green eyes could slice like a razor, and now was one of those times. "That sounds like a weather report," he said in an even tone. "Care to give me a percentage? Forty percent chance of matrimony? Fifty?"

"I don't know. I won't know until I meet the man."

He had been forking the pasta onto his plate, but now he carefully laid the utensils down and took a deep breath. Madelyn watched him with interest. It was one of the very few times when she could say she had seen Robert actually surprised.

He said, very carefully, "Do you mean you haven't met him yet?"

"No. We've corresponded, but we've never actually met. And we might not like each other in person. There's only a very small chance of matrimony, actually. In weather terms, no accumulation expected."

"But it's possible."

"Yes. I wanted you to know."

"How did you get to know him?"

"I don't know him. I know a little about him, but not much."

"So how did you start corresponding?"

"He advertised for a wife."

He looked stunned, really stunned. Madelyn took pity on him and ladled the thick, spicy sauce over his pasta before it grew cold, since it looked as if he had totally forgotten about it.

"You answered a personal ad?" he finally asked in a strained voice.

She nodded and turned her attention to her own plate. "Yes."

"Good God, do you know how risky that is?" he roared, half rising from his chair.

"Yes, I know." She reached over to pat his hand. "Please sit down and eat. You wouldn't panic if I'd told you I'd met someone at a singles bar in Manhattan, and that's a lot riskier than meeting a rancher from Montana."

"From a health viewpoint, yes, but there are other things to consider. What if this man is abusive? What if he has a criminal record, or is a con man? Just how much *do* you know about him?"

"He's your age, thirty-four. He owns a ranch in central Montana, and he's divorced, no children. I've been writing to a box number in Billings."

From the sharp look in Robert's eyes, Madelyn knew that he had made a mental note of everything she'd told him and wouldn't forget a single detail. She also knew that he would have Reese Duncan thoroughly investigated; she thought of protesting, but decided that it wouldn't make any difference. By the time Robert had his report, she would already have met Mr. Duncan and formed her own opinion. She could even see why Robert felt alarmed and protective, though she didn't agree that there was any need for it. Mr. Duncan's blunt correspondence had reassured her that this was a man who dealt in the unvarnished truth and didn't give a damn how it looked or sounded. It was relaxing not to have to gauge the sincerity of a come-on line.

"Can I talk you out of going?" Robert asked. "Or at least into delaying your meeting?"

"No." She smiled, her gray eyes aglow with anticipation. "I'm so curious I can hardly stand it."

He sighed. Madelyn was as curious as a cat, in her own lazy way. She didn't scurry around poking her nose into every new detail that came her way, but she would eventually get around to investigating any subject or situation that intrigued her. He could see where an ad for a wife would have been irresistible to her; once she had read it, it would have been a foregone conclusion that she had to meet the man for herself. If there was no way he could talk her out of going, he could make certain she wouldn't be in danger. Before she got on that plane, he would know if this Reese Duncan had any sort of criminal record, even so much as a parking ticket. If there was any indication that Madelyn wouldn't be perfectly safe, he would keep her off the flight if he had to sit on her.

As if she'd read his mind, she leaned forward. She had that angelic expression again, the one that made him wary. When Madelyn was angelic, she was either blisteringly angry or up to mischief, and he could never tell which until it was too late. "If you interfere in my social life, I'll assume that I have the same freedom with yours," she said sweetly. "In my opinion, you need a little help with your women."

She meant it. She never bluffed, never threatened unless she was prepared to carry through on her threats. Without a word, Robert tugged his white handkerchief out of his pocket and waved it in surrender.

2

The flight was a bit early landing in Billings. Madelyn carefully scrutinized the small group of people waiting to greet those leaving the plane, but she didn't see any lone males who appeared to be looking for her. She took a deep breath, glad of the small reprieve. She was unexpectedly nervous.

She used the time to duck into the ladies' room; when she came out, she heard her name being called in a tinny voice. "Madelyn Patterson, please meet your party at the Information desk. Madelyn Patterson, please meet your party at the Information desk."

Her heart was beating a little fast, but not unpleasantly so. She liked the feeling of excitement. The moment was finally at hand. Anticipation and curiosity were killing her.

She walked with an easy stride that was more of a stroll than anything else, despite her excitement. Her eyes were bright with pleasure. The Billings airport, with its big fountain, was more attractive than the general run of airports, and she let the surroundings begin to soothe her. She was only a little nervous now, and even that small bit wasn't revealed.

That must be him, leaning against the Information desk. He was wearing a hat, so she couldn't see his face all that well, but he was trim and fit. A smile quirked her mouth. This was a truly impossible situation. A real wild goose chase. They would meet, be polite, spend a polite day together; then tomorrow she would shake his hand and tell him she had enjoyed the visit, and that would be the end of it. It would all be very civil and low-keyed, just the way she liked—

He straightened from his relaxed position against the desk and turned toward her. Madelyn felt his eyes focus on her and grow intent.

She knew the meaning of the word *poleaxed*, but this was the first time she had ever experienced the feeling. Her lazy walk faltered, then stopped altogether. She stood frozen in the middle of the airport, unable to take another step. This had never happened to her before, this total loss of composure, but she was helpless. She felt stunned, as if she'd been kicked in the chest. Her heart was racing now, pounding out a painful rhythm. Her breath came in short, shallow gasps; her carry-on bag slipped out of her fingers and landed on the floor with a soft thud. She felt like a fool, but didn't really care. She couldn't stop staring at him.

It was just old-fashioned lust, that was all. It couldn't be anything else, not at first sight. She felt panic at the very idea that it could be anything else. Just lust.

He wasn't the most handsome man she'd ever seen, because New York was full of gorgeous men, but it didn't matter. In all the ways that did matter, all the primitive, instinctual ways, call it chemistry or electricity or biology or whatever, he was devastating. The man oozed sex. Every move he made was imbued with the sort of sensuality and masculinity that made her think of sweaty skin and twisted sheets. Dear God, why on earth should this man ever have had to advertise for a wife?

He was at least six-three, and muscled with the iron, layered strength of a man who does hard physical labor every day of his life. He was very tanned, and his hair, what she could see of it under his hat, was dark brown, almost black. His jaw was strongly shaped, his chin square, his mouth clear-cut and bracketed by twin grooves. He hadn't dressed up to meet her, but was wearing a plain white shirt with the cuffs unbuttoned and rolled back, ancient jeans and scuffed boots. She found herself frantically concentrating on the details of his appearance while she tried to deal with the havoc he was wreaking on her senses, all without saying a word.

None of her excited imaginings had prepared her for this. What was a woman supposed to do when she finally met the man who turned her banked coals into a roaring inferno? Madelyn's first thought was to run for her life, but she couldn't move.

Reese's first thought was that he'd like to take her to bed, but there was no way he'd take her to wife.

She was everything he'd been afraid she would be: a chic, sophisticated city woman, who knew absolutely nothing about a ranch. It was obvious from the top of her silky blond head down to the tips of her expensive shoes.

She was wearing white, not the most practical color for travel, but she was immaculate, without even a wrinkle to mar her appearance. Her skirt was pencil-slim and stopped just above her knees, revealing knockout legs. Reese felt his guts tighten, just looking at her legs. He wrenched his gaze upward with an effort that almost hurt and was struck by her eyes.

Beneath the loose, matching jacket she was wearing a skimpy top in a rich blue color that should have made her eyes look blue, but didn't. Her eyes made him feel as if he were drowning. They were gray, very gray, without a tinge of blue. Soft-looking eyes, even now when they were large with . . . dismay? He wasn't certain of the expression, but belatedly he realized that she was very pale and still, and that she'd dropped her bag.

He stepped forward, seizing on the excuse to touch her. He curved his hand around her upper arm, which felt cool and slim under his warm palm. "Are you all right? Miss Patterson?"

Madelyn almost shuddered at his touch, her response to it was so strong. How could such a small thing produce such an upheaval? His closeness brought with it the animal heat of his body, the scent of him, and she wanted to simply turn into his arms and bury her face against his neck. Panic welled up in her. She had to get out of here, away from him. She hadn't bargained on this. But instead of running, she called on all her reserves of control and even managed to smile as she held out her hand. "Mr. Duncan."

Her voice had a small rasp to it that tugged at him. He shook her hand, noting the absence of jewelry except for the plain gold hoops in her ears. He didn't like to see a woman's hands weighted down with rings on every finger, especially when the hands were as slim as hers. He didn't release her as he repeated, "Are you all right?"

Madelyn blinked, a slow closing and opening of her eyelids that masked a deep shifting and settling inside. "Yes, thank you," she replied, not bothering to make an excuse for her behavior. What could she say? That she'd been stunned by a sudden surge of lust for him? It was the truth, but one that couldn't be voiced. She knew she should be charming to ease the awkwardness of this meeting, but somehow she couldn't summon up the superficial chatter to gloss things over. She could do nothing but stand there.

They faced each other like gunfighters on a dirt street, oblivious to the eddies of people stepping around their small, immobile island. He was watching her from beneath level brows, taking his time with his survey but keeping his thoughts hidden. Madelyn stood still, very aware of her femaleness as he looked her up and down with acutely masculine appraisal, though he revealed neither appreciation nor disapproval. His thoughts were very much his own, his face that of an intensely private man.

Even shadowed by his hat brim as they were, she could tell that his eyes were a dark green-blue-hazel color, shot through with white striations that made them gleam. They were wrinkled at the outer corners from what must have been years of squinting into the sun, because he sure didn't look as if he'd gotten those lines from laughing. His face was stern and unyielding, making her long to see how he'd look if he smiled, and wonder if he had ever been carefree. This man wasn't a stranger to rough times or hard work.

"Let's go fetch your other luggage," he said, breaking the silent confrontation. It was a long drive back to the ranch, and he was impatient to be on the way. Chores had to be done no matter how late he got back.

His voice was a baritone, a bit gravelly. Madelyn registered the rough texture of it even as she nodded toward the carry-on bag. "That's it."

"All of it?"

"Yes."

If all her clothes were in that one small bag, she sure hadn't made any big plans to impress him with her wardrobe, he thought wryly. Of course, she would impress him most without any wardrobe at all.

He bent down to lift the carry-on, still keeping his hand on her arm. She was pure, walking provocation, totally unsuitable for ranch life, but every male hormone in him was clanging alert signals. She was only going to be here for a day; why shouldn't he enjoy being with her? It would be sort of a last fling before settling down with someone better prepared for the job, and job it would be. Ranching was hard work, and Madelyn Patterson didn't look as if she had ever been exposed to the concept.

Right now, though, he didn't mind, because she was so damn enticing and he was dead tired of the relentless months—years—of sixteen-hour days and backbreaking work. He would take her out to eat tonight, after his chores were done; maybe they'd go to Jasper's for some dancing, and he'd hold her in his arms for a while, feel the softness of her skin, smell her perfume. Who knew, maybe when they went back to the ranch it wouldn't be to separate beds. He'd have to be up front in telling her that she wasn't right for the job, so there wouldn't be any misunderstanding, but maybe it wouldn't make any difference to her. Maybe.

His hand naturally moved from her arm to her back as he led her out of the terminal. Deliberately he set about charming her, something he had once done with women as effortlessly as he had smiled. Those days were far in the past, but the touch remained. She chatted easily, thank God, asking questions about Montana, and he answered them just as easily, letting her relax and get comfortable with him, and all the while he studied her face and expressions.

Strictly speaking, she was merely pretty, but her face was lit by a liveliness that made her stunningly attractive. Her nose had a slight bump in it and was just a tiny bit crooked. A light dusting of freckles covered the bridge of it and scattered across her cheekbones, which were exquisitely chiseled. World-class cheekbones, just like her legs. Her lips weren't full, but her mouth was wide and mobile, as if she were forever on the verge of smiling. Her eyes were the grayest eyes he'd ever seen. They were calm, sleepy eyes that nevertheless revealed on closer inspection an alert and often amused intelligence, though he didn't see what she found so amusing.

If he'd met her before his rotten marriage and disastrous divorce, he would have gone after her like gangbusters, and gotten her, too, by God. Just the thought of those legs wrapped around his waist brought him to instant, uncomfortable arousal. No way, though, would he let his gonads lead him into another unsuitable marriage. He knew what he wanted in a wife, and Madelyn wasn't it. She didn't look as if she'd ever even seen a steer.

None of that decreased his physical response to her one whit. He'd been attracted to a lot of women at first sight, but not like this, not like a slam in the gut. This wasn't just attraction, a mild word to describe a mild interest; this was strong and wrenching, flooding his body with heat, making him grow hard even though he sure as hell didn't want to here in the middle of the airport. His hands actually hurt from wanting to touch her, to smooth over her breast and hip in a braille investigation of those sleek curves.

He felt a twinge of regret that she was so out of place, so totally unsuitable for his purposes. Walking beside her, he saw the sidelong glances that other men were giving her. Women like her just naturally attracted male speculation, and he wished he could afford to keep her, but she was too expensive for him. Reese was broke now, but at one time he had been accustomed to money; he knew how it looked and smelled and tasted, and how it fit. It fit Madelyn Patterson as perfectly as her silky skin did. She was slim and bright in her Paris-made suit, and the perfume sweetened by her warm flesh cost over two hundred dollars an ounce. He knew because it was one of his favorites. He couldn't even afford to keep her in perfume, much less clothes.

"What sort of work do you do?" he asked as they stepped into the bright sunshine. Those terse little letters she'd written hadn't revealed much.

She made a face, wrinkling her nose. "I work in an office without a window, doing nothing important, in my stepbrother's company. It's one of those jobs made for family." She didn't tell him that she'd turned in her notice, because he might assume she had done it thinking that she would be moving to Montana, and the one had nothing to do with the other. But her racing pulse told her that if he asked, she'd be packed and moved in with him so fast he'd think she owned her own moving company.

"Have you ever been on a ranch?" He asked it even though he already knew the answer.

"No." Madelyn looked up at him, something she still had to do despite her three-inch heels. "But I do know how to ride." She was actually a very good horsewoman, courtesy of her college roommate in Virginia, who had been horse mad.

He dismissed any riding she might have done. Recreational riding was a far cry from riding a workhorse, and that was what his horses were, trained and as valuable in their own way as a racehorse. It was just one more area where she didn't measure up.

They reached his truck, and he watched to see if she turned up her nose at it, as dusty and battered as it was. She didn't blink an eye, just stood to the side while he unlocked the door and placed her bag on the middle of the seat. Then he stepped back for her to get in.

Madelyn tried to seat herself and found that she couldn't. An astonished expression crossed her face; then she began to laugh as she realized her skirt was too tight. She couldn't lift her legs enough to climb up on the seat. "What women won't do for vanity," she said in a voice full of humor at her own expense and began tugging up the hem of the skirt. "I wore this because I wanted to look nice, but it would have been smarter to have worn slacks."

Reese's throat locked as he watched her pull up the skirt, exposing increasing amounts of her slim thighs. Heat exploded through him, making him feel as if his entire body were expanding. The thought flashed through his mind that he wouldn't be able to stand it if she pulled that skirt up one more inch, and in the next split second his hands shot out, catching her around the waist and lifting her onto the seat. She gave a startled little cry at his abrupt movement and grabbed his forearms to brace herself.

His mouth was dry, and sweat beaded on his forehead. "Don't pull up your skirt around me again, unless you want me to do something about it," he said in a guttural tone. His pulse was throbbing through him. She had the best legs he'd ever seen, long and strong, with sleek muscles. She'd be able to lock them around him and hang on, no matter how wild the ride.

Madelyn couldn't speak. Tension stretched between them, heavy and dark. Fierce, open lust burned in his narrowed eyes, and she couldn't look away, caught in the silent intensity. She was still gripping his forearms, and she felt the heat of his arms, the steely muscles bunched iron-hard under her fingers. Her heart lurched at the sharp realization that he felt some of the turmoil she had been feeling.

She began babbling an apology. "I'm sorry. I didn't intend—that is, I didn't realize—" She stopped, because she couldn't come right out and say that she hadn't meant to arouse him. No matter how she reacted to him, he was still essentially a stranger.

He looked down at her legs, with the skirt still halfway up them, and his hands involuntarily tightened on her waist before he forced himself to release her. "Yeah, I know. It's all right," he muttered. His voice was still hoarse. It wasn't all right. Every muscle in his body was tight. He stepped back before he could give in to the impulse to move forward instead, putting himself between her legs and opening them wider. All he would have to do would be to slide his hands under the skirt to push it up the rest of the way— He crushed the thought, because if he'd let himself finish it, his control would have shattered.

They had left Billings far behind before he spoke again. "Are you hungry? If you are, there's a café at the crossroads up ahead."

"No, thank you," Madelyn replied a bit dreamily as she stared at the wide vista of countryside around her. She was used to enormous buildings, but suddenly they seemed puny in comparison with this endless expanse of earth and sky. It made her feel both insignificant and fresh, as if her life were just starting now. "How far is it to your ranch?"

"About a hundred and twenty miles. It'll take us almost three hours to get there."

She blinked, astonished at the distance. She hadn't realized how much effort it was for him to come to Billings to meet her. "Do you go to Billings often?"

He glanced at her, wondering if she was trying to find out how much he isolated himself on the ranch. "No," he said briefly.

"So this is a special trip?"

"I did some business this morning, too." He'd stopped by the bank to give his loan officer the newest figures on the ranch's projected income for the coming year. Right now, it looked better than it had in a long time. He was still flat broke, but he could see daylight now. The banker had been pleased.

Madelyn looked at him with concern darkening her gray eyes. "So you've been on the road since about dawn."

"About that."

"You must be tired."

"You get used to early hours on a ranch. I'm up before dawn every day."

She looked around again. "I don't know why anyone would stay in bed and miss dawn out here. It must be wonderful."

Reese thought about it. He could remember how spectacular the dawns were, but it had been a long while since he'd had the time to notice one. "Like everything else, you get used to them. I know for a fact that there are dawns in New York, too."

She chuckled at his dry tone. "I seem to remember them, but my apartment faces to the west. I see sunsets, not dawns."

It was on the tip of his tongue to say that they would watch a lot of dawns together, but common sense stopped him. The only dawn they would have in common would be the next day. She wasn't the woman he would choose for a wife.

He reached into his shirt pocket and got out the pack of cigarettes that always resided there, shaking one free and drawing it the rest of the way out with his lips. As he dug in his jeans pocket for his lighter he heard her say incredulously, "You *smoke*?"

Swift irritation rose in him. From the tone of her voice you would have thought she had caught him kicking puppies, or something else equally repulsive. He lit the cigarette and blew smoke into the cab. "Yeah," he said. "Do you mind?" He made it plain from *his* tone of voice that, since it was his truck, he was damn well going to smoke in it.

Madelyn faced forward again. "If you mean, does the smoke bother me, the answer is no. I just hate to see anyone smoking. It's like playing Russian roulette with your life."

"Exactly. It's my life."

She bit her lip at his curtness. Great going, she thought. That's a good way to get to know someone, attack his personal habits.

"I'm sorry," she apologized with sincerity. "It's none of my business, and I shouldn't have said anything. It just startled me."

"Why? People smoke. Or don't you associate with anyone who smokes?"

She thought a minute, treating his sarcastic remark seriously. "Not really. Some of our clients smoke, but none of my personal friends do. I spent a lot of time with my grandmother, and she was very old-fashioned about the vices. I was taught never to swear, smoke or drink spirits. I've never smoked," she said righteously.

Despite his irritation, he found himself trying not to laugh. "Does that mean you swear and drink spirits?"

"I've been known to be a bit aggressive in my language in moments of stress," she allowed. Her eyes twinkled at him. "And Grandma Lily thought it was perfectly suitable for a lady to take an occasional glass of wine, medicinally, of course. During my college days, I also swilled beer."

"Swilled?"

"There's no other word to describe a college student's drinking manners."

Remembering his own college days, he had to agree.

"But I don't enjoy spirits," she continued. "So I'd say at least half of Grandma Lily's teachings stuck. Not bad odds."

"Did she have any rules against gambling?"

Madelyn looked at him, her mouth both wry and tender, gray eyes full of a strange acceptance. "Grandma Lily believed that life is a gamble, and everyone has to take their chances. Sometimes you bust, sometimes you break the house." It was an outlook she had passed on to her granddaughter. Otherwise, Madelyn thought, why would she be sitting here in a pickup truck, in the process of falling in love with a stranger?

It had been a long time since Reese had seen his home through the eyes of a stranger, but as he stopped the truck next to the house, he was suddenly, bitterly ashamed. The paint on the house was badly chipped and peeling, and the outbuildings were even worse. Long ago he'd given up trying to keep the yard neat and had finally destroyed the flower beds that had once delineated the house, because they had been overrun with weeds. In the past seven years nothing new had been added, and nothing broken had been replaced, except for the absolute necessities. Parts for the truck and tractor had come before house paint. Taking care of the herd had been more important than cutting the grass or weeding the flower beds. Sheer survival hadn't left time for the niceties of life. He'd done what he'd had to do, but that didn't mean he had to like the shape his home was in. He hated for Madelyn to see it like this, when it had once been, if not a showplace, a house no woman would have been ashamed of.

Madelyn saw the peeling paint, but dismissed it; after all, it wasn't anything that a little effort and several gallons of paint wouldn't fix. What caught her attention was the shaded porch, complete with swing, that wrapped all the way around the two-story house. Grandma Lily had had a porch like that, and a swing where they had whiled away many a lazy summer day to the accompaniment of the slow creak of the chains as they gently swayed.

"It reminds me of Grandma Lily's house," she said, her eyes dreamy again.

He opened her door and put his hands on her waist, lifting her out of the truck before she could slide to the ground. Startled all over again, she quickly looked up at him.

"I wasn't taking any chances with that skirt," he said, almost growling.

Her pulse began thudding again.

He reached inside the truck and hooked her carry-on bag with one hand, then took her arm with the other. They entered by the back door, which was unlocked. She was struck by the fact that he felt safe in not locking his door when he was going to be gone all day.

The back door opened into a combination mud-room and laundry. A washer and dryer lined the wall to the left, and the right wall bristled with pegs from which hung an assortment of hats, coats, ponchos and bright yellow rain slickers. A variety of boots, most of them muddy, were lined up on a rubber mat. Straight ahead and across a small hall was a full bathroom, which she realized would be convenient when he came in muddy from head to foot. He could take a bath without tracking mud or dripping water all through the house to the bathroom upstairs.

They turned left and were in the kitchen, a big, open, sunny room with a breakfast nook. Madelyn looked with interest at the enormous appliances, which didn't fit her image of what the kitchen of a small-scale, bachelor rancher should look like. She had expected something smaller and much more old-fashioned than this efficient room with its institutional-sized appliances.

"The house has ten rooms," he said. "Six downstairs, and four bedrooms upstairs."

"It's a big house for just one person," she commented, following him upstairs.

"That's why I want to get married." He made the comment as if explaining why he wanted a drink of water. "My parents built this house when I was a baby. I grew up here. I want to pass it on to my own children."

She felt a little breathless, and not just from climbing the stairs. The thought of having his children weakened her.

He opened a door directly across from the top of the stairs and ushered her into a large, pleasant bedroom with white curtains at the windows and a white bedspread on the four-poster bed. She made a soft sound of pleasure. An old rocking chair sat before one of the windows, and what was surely a handmade rug covered the smooth, hardwood plank flooring. The flooring itself was worth a small fortune. For all the charm of the room, there was a sense of bareness to it, no soft touches to personalize it in any way. But he lived here alone, she reminded herself; the personal touches would be in the rooms he used, not in the empty bedrooms waiting for his children to fill them.

He stepped past her and put her bag on the bed. "I can't take the whole day off," he said. "The chores have to be done, so I'll have to leave you to entertain yourself for a while. You can rest or do whatever you want. The bathroom is right down the hall if you want to freshen up. My bedroom has a private bath, so you don't have to worry about running into me."

In the space of a heartbeat she knew she didn't want to be left alone to twirl her fingers for the rest of the day. "Can't I go with you?"

"You'll be bored, and it's dirty work."

She shrugged. "I've been dirty before."

He looked at her for a long moment, his face unsmiling and expressionless. "All right," he finally said, wondering if she'd feel the same when her designer shoes were caked with the makings of compost.

Her smile crinkled her eyes. "I'll be changed in three minutes flat."

He doubted it. "I'll be in the barn. Come on out when you're ready."

As soon as he had closed the door behind him, Madelyn stripped out of her clothes, slithered into a pair of jeans and shoved her feet into her oldest pair of loafers, which she had brought along for this very purpose. After all, she couldn't very well explore a ranch in high heels. She pulled a white cotton cami-

sole on over her head and sauntered out the door just
as he was starting downstairs after changing shirts
himself. He gave her a startled look; then his eyes took
on a heavy-lidded expression as his gaze swept her
throat and shoulders, left bare by the sleeveless camisole. Madelyn almost faltered as that very male look
settled on her breasts, and her body felt suddenly
warm and weighed down. She had seen men cast quick
furtive glances at her breasts before, but Reese was
making no effort to hide his speculation. She felt her
nipples tingle and harden, rasping against the cotton
covering them.

"I didn't think you'd make it," he said.

"I don't fuss about clothes."

She didn't have to, he thought. The body she put
inside them was enough; anything else was superflu-
ous. He was all but salivating just thinking of her
breasts and those long, slender legs. The jeans covered them, but now he knew exactly how long and
shapely they were, and, as she turned to close the
bedroom door, how curved her buttocks were, like an
inverted heart. He felt a lot hotter than the weather
warranted.

She walked beside him out to the barn, her head
swiveling from side to side as she took in all the as-
pects of the ranch. A three-door garage in the same
style as the house stood behind it. She pointed to it.
"How many other cars do you have?"

"None," he said curtly.

Three other buildings stood empty, their windows
blank. "What are those?"

"Bunkhouses."

There was a well-built chicken coop, with fat white chickens pecking industriously around the yard. She said, "I see you grow your own eggs."

From the corner of her eye she saw his lips twitch as if he'd almost smiled. "I grow my own milk, too."

"Very efficient. I'm impressed. I haven't had fresh milk since I was about six."

"I didn't think that accent was New York City. Where are you from originally?"

"Virginia. We moved to New York when my mother remarried, but I went back to Virginia for college."

"Your parents were divorced?"

"No. My father died. Mom remarried three years later."

He opened the barn door. "My parents died within a year of each other. I·don't think they could exist apart."

The rich, earthy smell of an occupied barn enveloped her, and she took a deep breath. The odors of animals, leather, manure, hay and feed all mixed into that one unmistakable scent. She found it much more pleasant than the smell of exhaust.

The barn was huge. She had noticed a stable beside it, also empty, as well as a machinery shed and a hay shed. Everything about the ranch shouted that this had once been a very prosperous holding, but Reese had evidently fallen on hard times. How that must grate on a man with his obvious pride. She wanted to put her hand in his and tell him that it didn't matter, but she had the feeling he would reject the gesture. The pride that kept him working this huge place alone wouldn't allow him to accept anything he could interpret as pity.

She didn't know what chores needed doing or how to do them, so she tried to stay out of his way and simply watch, noting the meticulous attention he paid to everything he did. He cleaned out stalls and put down fresh hay, his powerful arms and back flowing with muscles. He put feed in the troughs, checked and repaired tack, brought in fresh water. Three horses were in a corral between the barn and stable; he checked and cleaned their hooves, brought them in to feed and water them, then put them in their stalls for the night. He called a ridiculously docile cow to him and put her in a stall, where she munched contentedly while he milked her. With a bucket half full of hot, foaming milk, he went back to the house, and two cats appeared to meow imperiously at him as they scented the milk. "Scat," he said. "Go catch a mouse."

Madelyn knew what to do now. She got the sterilized jugs she had noticed on her first trip through the kitchen and found a straining cloth. He gave her a strange look as she held the straining cloth over the mouth of the jug for him to pour the milk through. "Grandma Lily used to do this," she said in a blissful tone. "I was never strong enough to hold the bucket and pour, but I knew I'd be an adult the day she let me pour out the milk."

"Did you ever get to pour it?"

"No. She sold the cow the summer before I started school. She just had the one cow, for fresh milk, but the area was already building up and becoming less rural, so she got rid of it."

He set the bucket down and took the straining cloth. "Then here's your chance for adulthood. Pour."

A whimsical smile touched her lips as she lifted the bucket and carefully poured the creamy white liquid through the cloth into the jug. The warm, sweet scent filled the kitchen. When the bucket was empty she set it aside and said, "Thank you. As a rite of passage, that beats the socks off of getting my driver's license."

This time it happened. Reese's eyes crinkled, and his lips moved in a little half grin. Madelyn felt more of that inner shifting and settling, and knew that she was lost.

3

"There isn't much nightlife around, but there is a beer joint and café about twenty miles from here if you'd like to go dancing."

Madelyn hesitated. "Would you mind very much if we just stayed here? You must be tired, and I know I am. I'd rather put my feet up and relax."

Reese was silent. He hadn't expected her to refuse, and though he was tired, he'd been looking forward to holding her while they danced. Not only that, having people around them would dilute his focus on her, ease the strain of being alone with her. She wasn't right for him, damn it.

On the other hand, he'd been up since four that morning, and relaxing at home sounded like heaven. The hard part would be relaxing with her anywhere around.

"We could play Monopoly. I saw a game in the bookcase," she said. "Or cards. I know how to play poker, blackjack, spades, hearts, rummy, Shanghai, Spite and Malice, Old Maid and Go Fish."

He gave her a sharp glance at that improbable list. She looked as innocent as an angel. "I lost my Old Maid cards, but we can play rummy."

"Jokers, two-eyed jacks, threes, fives, sevens and Rachel are wild," she said promptly.

"On the other hand, there's a baseball game on television tonight. What the hell is a rachel?"

"It's the queen of diamonds. They have names, you know."

"No, I didn't know. Are you making that up?"

"Nope. Rachel is the queen of diamonds, Palas is the queen of spades, Judith is the queen of hearts, and Argine is the queen of clubs."

"Do the kings and jacks have names?"

"I don't know. That little bit of information has never come my way."

He eyed her again, then leaned back on the couch and propped his boots on the coffee table. She saw a hint of green gleam in his eyes as he said, "The little plastic doohickey on the end of your shoelaces is called an aglet."

She mimicked his position, her lips quirking with suppressed laughter. "The dimple in the bottom of a champagne bottle is called a punt."

"The empty space between the bottle top and the liquid is called ullage."

"A newly formed embryo is called a zygote."

"Bird's nest soup is made from the nests of swiftlets, which make the nests by secreting a glutinous substance from under their tongues."

Madelyn's eyes rounded with fascination, but she rose to the challenge. "Pink flamingos are pink because they eat so many shrimp."

"It takes light from the sun eight minutes and twenty seconds to reach earth."

"The common housefly flies at the speed of five miles an hour."

"An ant can lift fifty times its own weight."

She paused and eyed him consideringly. "Were you lying about the bird nests?"

He shook his head. "Are you giving up?"

"Never use all your ammunition in the opening salvo."

There wouldn't be much opportunity for follow-up salvos, he thought. In about eighteen hours he'd be putting her on a plane back to New York and they would never meet again.

The silence that fell between them was a little awkward. Madelyn got up and smiled at him. "I'll leave you to your baseball game, if you don't mind. I want to sit on the porch swing and listen to the frogs and crickets."

Reese watched her as she left the room, her hips rolling in a lazy sway. After a minute he heard the squeak of the chains as she sat down in the swing; then the creaking as she began pushing it back and forth. He turned on the television and actually watched a little of the ball game, but his mind was on the rhythmic creaking. He turned the television off.

Madelyn had been swinging and dreaming, her eyes closed, but she opened them when she heard the screen door open and close, then his boots on the wooden porch. He stopped a few feet away and leaned his shoulder against one of the posts.

His lighter flared; then the end of the cigarette glowed as it began to burn. Madelyn stared at his dim figure, wishing she had the right to get up and go to him, to slide her arms around his waist and rest her head on his shoulder. When he didn't speak, she closed her eyes again and began drifting in the peaceful darkness. The late spring night was comfortable, and the night creatures were going about their business as usual. This was the type of life she wanted, a life close to the earth, where serenity could be drawn from nature.

"Why did you answer the ad?"

His rough-textured voice was quiet, not disturbing the night. A few seconds passed before Madelyn opened her eyes and answered.

"For much the same reason you placed it, I suppose. Partly out of curiosity, I admit, but I also want to get married and have a family."

"You don't have to come all the way out here to do that."

She said, "Maybe I do," and was completely serious.

"You don't have any boyfriends in New York?"

"I have friends, yes, but no one I'm serious about, no one I'd want to marry. And I don't think I want to live in New York. This place is wonderful."

"You've only seen it at its best. Winter is frozen hell. Every place has its drawbacks."

"And its advantages. If you didn't think the positives outweighed the negatives, you wouldn't be here."

"I grew up here. This is my home. The Eskimos are attached to their homes, too, but I wouldn't live there."

Madelyn turned her head and looked out into the night, sensing what was coming and wishing, praying, that he wouldn't say it. She could tell from the way he'd been throwing up those subtle obstacles and objections what he was going to say.

"Madelyn. You don't fit in out here."

Her right foot kept up the slow, steady rhythm of the swing. "So the visit has been a failure?"

"Yes."

"Even though you're attracted to me?" In the darkness she could be bolder than she would have been otherwise. If faint heart ne'er won fair lady, she was sure that the fair lady ne'er won with a faint heart, either.

"The spark goes both ways." He stubbed out the cigarette on his boot heel and flipped it out into the yard.

"Yes. So why am I unsuitable for your purposes?"

"You're real suitable for the purposes of bed," he said grimly. "I'd like to take you there right now. But out of bed—no. You won't do at all."

"Please explain. I like to understand my rejections."

Suddenly he moved away from the post and sat next to her on the swing, setting it to dipping and swaying with his weight. One firmly planted boot took control of the motion and began the gentle rocking movement again.

"I was married before, for two years. You're like my first wife in a lot of ways. She was a city person. She liked the entertainment and variety of a big city. She'd never been on a ranch before, and thought it was romantic, just like a movie—until she realized that most of a rancher's time is spent working, instead of having a good time. She was already restless before winter came, and that just put the frosting on the cake. Our second year was pure hell."

"Don't judge me by someone else, Reese Duncan. Just because one woman didn't like it, doesn't mean another won't."

"A man who doesn't learn from his mistakes is a damn fool. When I marry again, it'll be to a woman who knows what ranch life is like, who'll be able to work with me. I won't risk the ranch again."

"What do you mean?"

"This ranch was once one of the biggest and best. You can tell by looking around you that it used to be a lot more than what it is now. I had the two best breeding bulls in four states, a good insemination program going, over four thousand head of beef, and fifty people working for me. Then I got divorced." He lifted his arm and rested it along the back of the swing. She could see only his profile, but even in the darkness she could make out the bitter line of his mouth, hear his bitterness in his voice. "April's family had a lot of influence with the judge. He agreed that two years as my wife entitled her to half of my assets, but she sweetly decided that a lump sum settlement would do just fine, thank you. I nearly went bankrupt. I had to liquidate almost everything to buy her off. I sold land that had been in my family for over a hundred years. That was seven years ago. I've been working my ass off since then just trying to keep this place going, and this year it looks like I'll finally make a profit again. I want kids, someone to leave the ranch to, but this time I'll make a better choice of woman."

She was appalled at the cause of his circumstances, but still said tartly, "What about love? How does that fit into your plans?"

"It doesn't," he replied in a flat tone.

"What if your wife wants more?"

"I don't plan to spin her a pretty story. She'll know where I stand from the first. But I'll be a good husband. I don't stray, or mistreat women. All I ask from a wife is loyalty and competence and the same values I have."

"And to be ready to stand as a brood mare."

"That too," he agreed.

Disappointment so sharp that it felt like a knife stabbed into her midsection. He was going to marry someone else. She looked away from him and reached deep for the control she needed. "Then I wish you luck. I hope you have a happy marriage this time. Do you have any more applicants?"

"Two more. If either of them is interested in ranch life, I'll probably ask her to marry me."

He had it as cut-and-dried as any business deal, which was all it was to him, even though he would be sleeping with his business partner. Madelyn could have cried at such a waste of passion, but she held on to her control. All she could do now was cut her losses and try to forget him, so she wouldn't measure every man she met against him for the rest of her life.

The darkness hid the desolation in her eyes as she said, "A jackrabbit can run as fast as a racehorse—for a short distance, of course."

He didn't miss a beat. "A group of bears is called a sloth."

"The Pacific Ocean covers almost sixty-four-million square miles."

"The safety pin was invented in 1849."

"No! That long ago? Zippers were invented in 1893,
and it's a good thing, because wouldn't you hate to get
caught in a safety pin?"

She was quiet on the drive back to Billings the next
morning. The evening had ended well, with the hilar-
ity of their mutual store of odd facts, but the strain
had told on her in the form of a sleepless night. She
couldn't bear the thought of never seeing him again,
but that was the way it was, and she was determined
to keep her pain to herself. Nothing would be gained
by weeping all over him, which was exactly what she
felt like doing.

He looked tired, too, and it was no wonder when she
considered how early he'd had to get up for the past
two days, and how much driving he'd done. She said,
"I'm sorry you're having to go to so much trouble to
take me back."

He shot her a glance before returning his attention
to the road. "You had a wasted trip, too."

So she was categorized under "Wasted Trip." She
wondered wryly if her other dates had merely been
flattering her all these years.

It was only about half an hour before her flight
when they reached the airport. He'd timed it nicely,
she thought. She wouldn't have to rush, but on the
other hand, there wasn't time for a lengthy goodbye,
and she was glad. She didn't know how much she
could take. "You don't need to park," she said. "Just
let me out."

He gave her another glance, but this one was
strangely angry. He didn't speak, just parked and
came around to open the door for her. Quickly she

jumped out before he could catch her by the waist and
lift her out again.

Reese's mouth had a grim set as he put his hand on
the small of her back and walked with her into the
terminal. At least the skirt she was wearing today was
full enough that she could move freely, but the way it
swung around her legs was just as maddening, in a
different way, as that tight white skirt had been. He
kept thinking that this one would be even easier to
push up out of the way.

Her flight was just being called when they reached
the gate. She turned with a smile that cost more than
she could afford and held out her hand. "Goodbye,
Reese. I wish you luck."

He took her hand, feeling the smooth texture of her
fingers in contrast to his hardened, callused palm. She
would be that smooth and silky all over, and that was
why he was sending her away. He saw her wide, soft
lips part as she started to say something else, and
hunger rose up in him like a tidal wave, crashing over
barriers and sweeping everything away.

"I have to taste you," he said in a low, harsh tone,
carrying her hand upward to tuck it around his neck.
"Just once." His other arm circled her waist and
pulled her to him as he bent his head.

It wasn't a polite goodbye kiss. It was hard and
deep. His mouth was hot and wild, with the taste of
tobacco and himself. Madelyn put her other arm
around his neck and hung on, because her legs had
gone watery. The force of his mouth opened hers, and
he took her with his tongue. He held her to him with
painful pressure, crushing her breasts against him and

cradling her pelvis against the hard, aching ridge of his manhood.

Vaguely she heard other people around them. It didn't matter. He was making love to her with his mouth, arousing her, satisfying her, consuming her. He increased the slant of his head, tucking her head more firmly into his shoulder, and kissed her with all the burning sensuality she had sensed in him on first sight.

Her heart lurched as pleasure overrode shock, swiftly escalating to an almost unbearable tension. She not only welcomed the intrusion of his tongue, she met it with her own, making love to him as surely as he was to her. He shuddered, and for a second his arms tightened so fiercely that she moaned into his mouth. Instantly they loosened, and he lifted his head.

Breathing swiftly, only inches apart, they stared at each other. His expression was hard and sensual, his eyes dilated with arousal, his lips still gleaming from the moisture of their kiss. He was bending back toward her when another call for her flight stopped him, and he slowly released her.

Her entire body ached for him. She waited, hoping he would say the words that would keep her there, but instead he said, "You'd better go. You'll miss your flight."

She couldn't speak. She nodded instead and walked away on shaky legs. She didn't look back. It was bad form for a grown woman to howl like an infant, and that was what she was very much afraid she would do if she gave in to the need to see him for even a split second.

She had gotten off the plane in Billings feeling confident and alive with anticipation. She left twenty-four hours later feeling shattered.

Robert met her plane in New York, which told Madelyn how worried he'd been. She gave him a parody of a smile and saw his pale eyes sharpen as he immediately read her distress. The smile wobbled and collapsed, and she walked into his arms. She didn't cry; she didn't let herself cry, but her chest heaved with convulsive breaths as she fought for control.

"I'll kill him," Robert said in a very soft, almost gentle tone.

Madelyn shook her head and took one more deep breath so she could talk. "He was a perfect gentleman. He's a hard-working, salt-of-the-earth type, and he said I wasn't suitable for the job."

He rocked her gently back and forth. "And that hurt your ego?"

She raised her head and managed a real smile this time, though it was just as wobbly as the first. "No, I think he managed to break my heart."

Robert gave her a searching look, reading the expression in her bottomless gray eyes. "You don't fall in love in one day."

"Sometimes you don't, sometimes you do. He didn't feel the same way, so it's something I have to live with."

"Maybe it's just as well." Keeping his arm around her shoulder, he guided her toward the entrance. "I investigated him—I know, you told me not to," he added warily as he saw the menacing look she gave him. "But he would be a tough man for any woman to live with. He's understandably bitter about the raw deal he got in his divorce—"

"I know," she said. "He told me about it."

"Then you know that any woman he marries will have a cold marriage. He's still carrying a lot of anger inside him."

"I saw the ranch. He has reason to be angry."

"His ex-wife and her family took him to the cleaners. I've dealt with them—cautiously. You have to be careful when you wade into a pool of barracudas."

"I'd like for you to ruin them financially, if you can, please," she said in the manner of a socialite idly asking for another glass of champagne.

"That won't give him back what he lost."

"No, but I'm vindictive enough that I want to see them get what they deserve."

"You don't have a vindictive bone in your body."

"Yes I do," she said in the same gentle tone he occasionally used, the one that made smart people back away.

He kissed her hair and hugged her closer. "So what are you going to do now?"

"Carry on, I suppose." She shrugged. "There's nothing else I can do."

Robert looked at her, wryly admiring her resilience. Madelyn was a trooper; she always carried on. Sometimes she needed a crutch for a while, but in the end she stood upright again and continued on her own. Reese Duncan had to be a lot of man to have gotten to her this way.

Two weeks later, Reese got back into his truck after seeing his latest visitor, Juliet Johnson, off on the bus.

He cursed and slammed his fist against the steering wheel, then lit a cigarette and began smoking it with fast, furious puffs.

This had all been a damn waste of time and money. The schoolteacher, Dale Quillan, had taken a good hard look at the isolation of the ranch and politely told him she wasn't interested. Miss Johnson, on the other hand, had been willing to take on the job, but he couldn't bring himself to make the offer. That was the sourest woman he'd ever met, humorless and disapproving of almost everything she saw. He'd imagined her as the family-oriented type, since she had sacrificed her life to care for her invalid mother, but now he figured she had been more of a cross than a blessing to the poor woman. She had informed him tartly that she would be willing to perform her duties by him once they were sanctified by marriage, but she hoped he didn't plan on a lot of foolish shenanigans because she didn't believe in such. Reese had told her just as sharply that he believed she could rest easy on that score.

Three applicants. One he wouldn't have, one wouldn't have him, and the other was all wrong for the job.

Madelyn. Long, beautiful legs. Silky blond hair and deep gray eyes. A soft mouth and a taste like honey. What would ranch life do to someone that elegant and unprepared?

But he'd spent two weeks turning his bed into a shambles every night because his frustrated body wouldn't let him sleep, and when he did manage to sleep he dreamed about her and woke up in even worse shape than when he'd dozed off. His loins ached, his temper was frayed, and he was smoking twice as much as normal. Damn her for being more than he wanted, or could afford.

She had clung to him and kissed him with such a fiery response that he hadn't been able to sleep at all that night, but she'd walked away from him without a backward glance. If she'd turned around just once, if she'd shown the least reluctance to go, he might have weakened and asked her to stay, but she hadn't. She'd even wished him good luck in finding a wife. It didn't sound as if his rejection had wounded her too badly.

He could have kept her. It drove him half-wild to know that she would have stayed if he'd asked her, that they could have been married by now. She would be lying under him every night, and the bed might get torn up, but it wouldn't be out of frustration.

No. She was too much like April. If he ever let her get her claws into him, she would rip him to shreds even worse than April had done, because even in the beginning he'd never been as hot to have April as he was to have Madelyn. She was used to city life, and though she'd appeared to like Montana and the ranch, the real test was living through a winter here. She'd never make it.

He ground out the cigarette and lit another, feeling the smoke burn his throat and lungs.

Fury and frustration boiled over. He got out of the truck and strode to a pay phone. A call to Information got her number. This was probably another waste of time; at this time of day she'd be at work, but he was driven by an urgency he bitterly resented and was still unable to resist.

He punched in her number, and an operator came on the line to tell him how much money to deposit. He dug in his pocket for change, swearing under his breath when he saw he didn't have enough.

"Sir, please deposit the correct amount."

"Just a minute." He got out his wallet and flipped through the papers until he found his telephone credit card and read off the account number to the operator. He hadn't used the card in seven years, so he hoped it was still good.

Evidently it was, because the operator said, "Thank you," and he heard the electronic beeps as the call went through.

It rang three times; then there was a click as the receiver was picked up and that warm, faintly raspy voice said, "Hello."

"Madelyn."

There was a pause; then she said, "Yes. Reese?"

"Yes." He stopped as a truck roared by, waiting until he could hear again. "You've been out here and seen what it's like. Are you willing to marry me?"

The pause this time was longer, and his fist tightened on the receiver until he thought the plastic might crack under the pressure. Finally she said, "The other two didn't work out?"

"No. What's your answer?"

"Yes," she said calmly.

He closed his eyes as the almost unbearable tension eased. God, he might be making a mistake as bad as the one he'd made with April, but he had to have her. "You'll have to sign a prenuptial agreement giving up all rights to the property I own prior to marriage and waiving any right to alimony or a lump sum settlement in case of divorce."

"All right. That's a mutual agreement, isn't it? What's yours remains yours and what's mine remains mine?"

Irritation lashed at him. "Of course."

"Fine, then."

"I want a certification from a doctor that you're in good health."

"All right. I require a certification from *your* doctor, as well."

The irritation threatened to become rage, but he held it in control. She had as much right to be reassured about his health as he did to be reassured about hers. Sexually transmitted diseases didn't stop at the Montana border, and AIDS wasn't the only concern people should have.

"I want the wedding within two weeks. When can you get out here?"

"How long is the waiting period?"

"Five days, I think. I'll have to check. Can you get here next week?"

"I think so. Give me your number and I'll call you."

He recited his phone number; then silence crackled along the line. He said, "I'll see you next week."

Another pause. Then, "Yes. I'll see you then. 'Bye."

He said goodbye and hung up, then leaned against the booth for a minute, his eyes closed. He'd done it. He'd asked her to marry him against all common sense, but this time he would protect himself and the ranch. He'd have her, but he'd keep her at a distance, and all the legal documents would keep the ranch safe.

He lit another cigarette and coughed as the acrid smoke stung his raw throat. In his mind's eye he saw her incredulous face when she'd looked at him and said, *"You smoke?"* He took the cigarette out of his mouth and looked at it; he'd smoked for years, and usually enjoyed it, but he'd been smoking too much lately.

You smoke?

Swearing again, he put out the cigarette. As he strode angrily back to the truck he passed a trash barrel, and without giving himself time to think he tossed the cigarette pack into it. He was still swearing as he got into the truck and started it. For a few days he was going to be in the mood to wrestle grizzlies, and he didn't look forward to it.

Madelyn slowly replaced the receiver, numb with shock. She couldn't believe he'd called. She couldn't believe she'd said she would marry him. She couldn't believe anything about their conversation. It had to be the most unromantic, businesslike, *insulting* proposal on record. And she'd still said yes. Yes! A thousand times *yes!*

She had to be in Montana in a week. She had a million things to do: get packed, get the apartment closed up, say goodbye to all her friends—and have a physical, of course. But all she could do right now was sit, her thoughts whirling.

She had to be practical. It was obvious Reese wasn't giving the marriage much of a chance, even though he was going into it for his own reasons. She wondered why the other two hadn't worked out, because he'd been so adamant that she was wrong for the job. But he wanted her, she knew, remembering that kiss at the airport and the way he'd looked at her. She wanted him, more than she'd ever thought it was possible to want a man, both physically and emotionally, but was that enough to hold together a relationship when they were faced with the day-in, day-out routine that marriage entailed? Would she still love him when he had a cold and was grouchy, or yelled at her for something that wasn't her fault? Would he still want her after he'd seen her without makeup, stumbling around in the morning with uncombed hair, or when she was in a bad mood, too?

Looking at it clearly, she decided that she should ask the doctor about birth control pills while she was there. If everything worked out and they decided to have children, it would be easy to go off the Pill, but what a mess it would be if she got pregnant right away and then the marriage fell apart. It was something she would already have discussed with Reese if their situation had been a normal one, but nothing about this was normal.

She was making a complete change in her life, from urban to rural, from single to marriage, all without really knowing the man she was marrying. She didn't know his favorite foods or colors, his moods, how he would react to any given situation; all she really knew about him was that his store of miscellaneous knowledge rivaled hers, and that she responded more violently to him than anyone she'd ever met before. She was definitely following her heart here, and not her head.

Reese would want the marriage ceremony to be conducted with as little fuss as possible, before a magistrate or a justice of the peace. She didn't mind that, but she made up her mind that Robert would be there, and her friend Christine. They could be the witnesses, rather than two strangers.

Robert was less than thrilled with the news, as she had expected. "I know you fell for him, but shouldn't you give this more time? You've met him once. Or did you get to know him *really* well during that one meeting?"

"I told you, he was a perfect gentleman."

"Ah, but were you a perfect lady?"

"I'm good at whatever I do, but I've never claimed to be perfect."

His eyes twinkled, and he leaned over to pinch her cheek. "You're determined to have this man, aren't you?"

"He gave me this chance, and I'm taking it before he changes his mind. Oh yes, we're getting married now if I have to kidnap him."

"He may be in for a surprise," Robert mused. "Does he know about that bulldog stubbornness you hide behind that lazy walk and talk?"

"Of course not. Give me some credit. He'll learn about that in due time, after we're married." She smiled that sweet smile.

"So, when do I get to meet him?"

"The day of the wedding, probably. No matter what you have scheduled, I expect you to drop everything and fly out when I call you."

"Wouldn't miss it."

Christine was even less encouraging. "What do you know about ranch life?" she asked ominously. "Nothing. There are no movies, no neighbors, not even any television reception to speak of. No plays, no operas or concerts."

"No pollution, no having to put six different locks on my door when I go out, no getting mugged when I go shopping."

"You've never been mugged."

"But there's always the possibility. I know people who've been mugged several times."

"There's the *possibility* of a lot of things. It's *possible* I may even get married some day, but I'm not holding my breath waiting. That isn't the point. You really have no idea what life on a ranch is like. At least I have *some* idea. It's a hard, lonely way to live, and you're not the isolated type."

"*Au contraire,* dear friend. I'm just as content by myself as I am surrounded by people. If I had to live in Outer Mongolia to be with him, I'd do it."

Christine looked amazed. "Ye gods," she blurted. "You're in love!"

Madelyn nodded. "Of course. Why else would I marry him?"

"Well, that explains the sudden madness. Does he feel the same way?"

"Not yet. I'm going to do my best to convince him, though."

"Would it be wasting my breath to point out that that usually comes *before* the part where you say 'I do'? That courtship usually covers this phase?"

Pursing her lips, Madelyn considered it, then said, "No, I think it would come more under 'falling on deaf ears' than 'wasting your breath.' I'm getting married. I'd like you to be there."

"Of course I'll be there! Nothing could keep me away. I have to see this paragon of manly virtues."

"I never said he was virtuous."

In complete understanding, they looked at each other and smiled.

4

They were married in Billings twelve days later. Madelyn was exhausted by the time of the wedding, which was performed in the judge's chambers. She had gotten only a few hours of sleep each night since Reese's phone call, because it had taken so much time to pack up a lifetime of belongings, sorting through and discarding what she wasn't taking, and packing what she couldn't bear to do without. She had also gotten the required physical and expressed the results to Reese, and hadn't been surprised when she had received his results by express mail the same day.

She had shipped numerous boxes containing books, albums, tapes, CDs, stereo equipment and winter clothes to the ranch, wondering what Reese would have to say about having his home taken over by the paraphernalia of a stranger. But when she'd spoken to him during two brief telephone calls he hadn't mentioned it. Before she knew it she was flying to Billings again, but this time she wasn't coming back.

Reese didn't kiss her when he met her at the airport, and she was glad. She was tired and on edge, and the first self-doubts were creeping in. From the look on his face, when he started kissing her again he didn't intend to stop, and she wasn't ready for that. But her heart leaped at the sight of him, reassuring her that she was doing the right thing.

She planned to stay at a motel in Billings for the five days until their marriage; Reese scowled at her when she told him her plan.

"There's no point in paying for a motel when you can stay at the ranch."

"Yes, there is. For one thing, most of my New York clothes are useless and will just stay packed up. I have to have Montana clothing—jeans, boots and the like. There's no point in making an extra trip later on to buy it when I'm here already. Moreover, I'm not staying alone with you right now, and you know why."

He put his hands on her waist and pulled her up against him. His narrowed eyes were dark green. "Because I'd have you under me as soon as we got in the house."

She swallowed, her slender hands resting on his chest. She could feel the heavy beat of his heart under her palms, a powerful pumping that revealed the sexual tension he was holding under control. "Yes. I'm not ready to start that part of our relationship. I'm tired, and nervous, and we really don't know each other that well—"

"We're getting married in five days. We won't know each other much better by then, baby, but I don't plan on spending my wedding night alone."

"You won't," she whispered.

"So one of the conditions for getting you in bed is to put a ring on your finger first?" His voice was getting harsher.

He was angry, and she didn't want him to be; she just wanted him to understand. She said steadily,

"That isn't it at all. If the wedding were two months away, or even just a month, I'm certain we'd...we'd make love before the ceremony, but it isn't. I'm just asking you for a little time to rest and recuperate first."

He studied her upturned face, seeing the translucent shadows under her eyes and the slight pale cast to her skin. She was resting against him, letting his body support hers, and despite his surging lust he realized that she really was tired. She had uprooted her entire life in just one week, and the emotional strain had to be as exhausting as the physical work.

"Then sleep," he said in a slow, deep voice. "Get a lot of sleep, baby, and rest up. You'll need it. I can wait five days—just barely."

She did get some sleep, but the emotional strain was still telling on her. She was getting married; it was natural to be nervous, she told herself.

The day they signed the prenuptial agreement at the lawyer's office was another day of stress. Reese was in a bad mood when he picked her up at the motel, growling and snapping at everything she said, so she lapsed into silence. She didn't think it was a very good omen for their marriage.

The prenuptial agreement was brief and easily understood. In case of divorce, they both kept the property and assets they had possessed prior to their marriage, and Madelyn gave up all rights to alimony in any form. She balked, however, at the condition that he retain custody of any children that should result from their union.

"No," she said flatly. "I'm not giving up my children."

Reese leaned back in the chair and gave her a look that would have seared metal. "You're not taking my children away from me."

"Calm down," the lawyer soothed. "This is all hypothetical. Both of you are talking as if a divorce is inevitable, and if that's the case, I would suggest that you *not* get married. Statistics say that half of new marriages end in divorce, but that means that half don't. You may well be married to each other for the rest of your lives, and there may not be any children anyway."

Madelyn ignored him. She looked only at Reese. "I don't intend to take our children away from you, but neither do I intend to give them up. I think we should share custody, because children need both parents. Don't try to make me pay for what April did," she warned.

"But you'd want them to live with you."

"Yes, I would, just as you'd want them to live with you. We aren't going to change that by negotation. If we did divorce, I'd never try to turn our children against you, nor would I take them out of the area, but that's something you'll just have to take on trust, because I'm not signing any paper that says I'll give up my children."

There were times, he noted, when those sleepy gray eyes could become sharp and clear. She was all but baring her teeth at him. It seemed there were some things that mattered enough to rouse her from her habitual lazy amusement, and it was oddly reassuring that the subject of their children, hypothetical though they were, was one of them. If he and April had had a child, she would have wanted custody of it only as a way to get back at him, not because she really wanted the child itself. April hadn't wanted to have children at all, a fact for which he was now deeply grateful. Madelyn not only appeared to want children, she was ready to fight for them even before they existed.

"All right," he finally said, and nodded to the lawyer. "Strike that clause from the agreement. If there's ever a divorce, we'll hash that out then."

Madelyn felt drained when they left the lawyer's office. Until then, she hadn't realized the depth of Reese's bitterness. He was so determined not to let another woman get the upper hand on him that it might not be possible for her to reach him at all. The realization that she could be fighting a losing battle settled on her shoulders like a heavy weight.

"When do your stepbrother and best friend get here?" he asked curtly. He hadn't liked the idea of Robert and Christine being at their wedding, and now Madelyn knew why. Having friends and relatives there made it seem more like a real wedding than just a business agreement, and a business agreement, with bed privileges, was all Reese wanted, all he could accept.

"The day before the wedding. They won't be able to stay afterward, so we're going out to a restaurant the night before. You can be here, can't you?"

"No. There's no one at the ranch to put the animals up for the night and do the chores for me. Even if I left immediately afterward, it's almost a three hour drive, so there's no point in it."

She flushed. She should have thought of the long drive and how hard he had to work. It was a sign of how much she had to learn about ranching. "I'm sorry, I should have thought. I'll call Robert—"

He interrupted her. "There's no reason why you should cancel just because I can't be here. Go out with them and enjoy it. We won't have much chance to eat out after we're married."

If he'd expected her to react with horror at that news, he was disappointed. She'd already figured that out on her own, and she didn't care. She intended to be his partner in rebuilding the ranch; maybe when it was prosperous again he could let go of some of his bitterness. She would gladly forego restaurant meals to accomplish that.

"If you're certain . . ."

"I said so, didn't I?" he snapped.

She stopped and put her hands on her hips. "I'd like to know just what your problem is! I've seen men with prostate problems and women with terminal PMS who aren't as ill-tempered as you. Have you been eating gunpowder or something?"

"I'll tell you what's wrong!" he roared. "I'm trying to quit smoking!" Then he strode angrily to the truck, leaving her standing there.

She blinked her eyes, and slowly a smile stretched her lips. She strolled to the truck and got in. "So, are you homicidal or merely as irritable as a wounded water buffalo?"

"About halfway in between," he said through clenched teeth.

"Anything I can do to help?"

His eyes were narrow and intense. "It isn't just the cigarettes. Take off your panties and lock your legs around me, and I'll show you."

She didn't want to refuse him. She loved him, and he needed her, even if it was only in a sexual way. But she didn't want their first time to be a hasty coupling in a motel room, especially when she was still jittery from stress and he was irritable from lack of nicotine. She didn't know if it would be any better by their wedding day, but she hoped she would be calmer.

He saw the answer in her eyes and cursed as he ran his hand around the back of his neck. "It's just two damn days."

"For both of us." She looked out the window. "I admit, I'm trying to put it off. I'm nervous about it."

"Why? I don't abuse women. If I don't have the control I need the first time, I will the second. I won't hurt you, Maddie, and I'll make certain you enjoy it."

"I know," she said softly. "It's just that you're still basically a stranger."

"A lot of women crawl into bed with men they've just met in a bar."

"*I* don't."

"Evidently you don't crawl into bed with the man you're going to marry, either."

She rounded on him. "That's unfair and you know it, because we aren't getting married under the usual circumstances. If you're not going to do anything but snap at me and try to pressure me into bed, maybe we shouldn't see each other until the wedding."

His teeth came together with a snap. "That sounds like a damn fine idea to me."

So she spent the last two days before her wedding alone, at least until Robert and Christine arrived the afternoon before. She hadn't expected Reese to drive to Billings every day, and in fact he hadn't, except to meet her at the airport and to go to the lawyer's office, but it disturbed her that they had already quarreled. If their marriage survived, it looked like it would be a tempestuous one.

When she met Christine and Robert at the airport, Christine looked around impatiently. "Well, where is he?"

"At the ranch, working. He doesn't have anyone to look after the animals, so he isn't coming in tonight."

Christine frowned, but to Madelyn's surprise Robert took it in stride. It only took a moment's thought to realize that if there was anything Robert understood, it was work coming before everything else.

She hooked her arms through theirs and hugged both of them. "I'm so glad you're here. How was the flight?"

"Exciting," Christine said. "I've never traveled with the boss before. He gets red-carpet treatment, did you know?"

"Exasperating," Robert answered smoothly. "She makes smartmouth comments, just like you do. I kept hearing those sotto voce remarks in my ear every time a flight attendant came by."

"They didn't just come by," Christine explained. "They stopped, they lingered, they swooned."

Madelyn nodded. "Typical." She was pleased that Christine wasn't intimidated by Robert, as so many people were. Christine would never have been so familiar in the office, and in fact Madelyn doubted that the two had ever met before, but in this situation he was merely the bride's brother and she was the bride's best friend, and she had treated him as such. It also said something about Robert's urbanity that Chris-

tine did feel at ease with him; when he chose, her
stepbrother could turn people to stone with his icy
manner.

Now if only her two favorite people in the world
would like the man she loved. She hoped he'd recovered from his nicotine fit by the morning, or it could
be an interesting occasion.

They took a cab to the motel where she was staying, and Robert got a room, but Madelyn insisted that
Christine stay in the room with her. On this last night
as a single woman, her nerves were frayed, and she
wanted someone to talk to, someone she could keep up
all night if she couldn't sleep herself. After all, she
reasoned, what were friends for if not to share misery?

They shared a pleasant meal and enjoyed themselves, though Madelyn wished Reese could have been
there. By ten o'clock Christine was yawning openly
and pointed out that it was midnight in New York.
Robert signaled for the check; he looked as fresh as he
had that morning, but he was used to working long
hours and usually only slept four hours a night anyway.

"Will you sleep tonight?" he asked Madelyn when
they got back to the motel, having noticed her shadowed eyes.

"Probably not, but I don't think a bride is supposed to sleep the night before she gets married."

"Honey, it's the night she gets married that she isn't
supposed to sleep."

She wrinkled her nose at him. "Then either. I'm
tired, but I'm too nervous and excited to sleep. It's
been that way since he called."

"You aren't having second thoughts?"

"Second, third and fourth thoughts, but it always comes back to the fact that I can't let this chance pass."

"You could always postpone it."

She thought of how impatient Reese was and wryly shook her head. "No, I couldn't, not one more day."

He hugged her close, resting his cheek on her bright head. "Then give it all you've got, honey, and he'll never know what hit him. But if it doesn't work out, don't punish yourself. Come home."

"I've never heard such a bunch of doubting Thomases before," she chided. "But thanks for the concern. I love you, too."

By the time she went inside, Christine was already crawling into bed. Madelyn picked up the pillow and hit her with it. "You can't sleep tonight. You have to hold my hand and keep me calm."

Christine yawned. "Buy some beer, get wasted and go to sleep."

"I'd have a hangover on my wedding day. I need sympathy, not alcohol."

"The most I can offer you is two aspirin. I'm too tired to offer sympathy. Besides, why are you nervous? You want to marry him, don't you?"

"Very much. Just wait until you see him, then you'll know why."

One of Christine's eyes opened a crack. "Intimidating?"

"He's very . . . male."

"Ah."

"Eloquent comment."

"It covered a lot of ground. What did you expect at—" she stopped to peer at her watch "—one o'clock in the morning? Shakespearean sonnets?"

"It's only eleven o'clock here."

"My body may be here, but my spirit is on Eastern Daylight Time. Good night, or good morning, whichever the case may be."

Laughing, Madelyn let Christine crash in peace. She got ready for bed herself, then lay awake until almost dawn, both mind and body tense.

The dress she had bought for the wedding was old-fashioned in design, almost to her ankles, with eyelet lace around the hem and neckline. She pinned up her hair in a modified Gibson girl, and put on white lace hosiery and white shoes. Even though it was just going to be a civil ceremony, she was determined to look like a bride. Now that the day had actually arrived she felt calm, and her hands were steady as she applied her makeup. Maybe she had finally gotten too tired for nervousness.

"You look gorgeous," said Christine, who looked pretty good herself in an ice-blue dress that did wonders for her olive complexion. "Cool and old-fashioned and fragile."

Fragile was a word Madelyn had never used to describe herself, and she turned to Christine in disbelief.

"I didn't say you *were* fragile, I said you *looked* fragile, which is just the way you're supposed to look on your wedding day."

"You have some interesting ideas. I know the something borrowed, something blue routine, but I always thought a bride was supposed to look radiant, not fragile.''

"Pooh. Radiance is easy. Just a few whisks with a blusher brush. Fragile is much harder to achieve. I'll bet you stayed up nights perfecting it."

Madelyn sighed and looked at herself in the mirror again. "I didn't think it showed."

"Did you sleep any?"

"An hour or so."

"It shows."

When Reese knocked on the door, Madelyn froze. She knew it was Reese, and not Robert. Her heart began that slow, heavy beat as she crossed the room to open the door.

Reese looked down at her, his expression shadowed by his gray dress Stetson. With his boots on he stood over six-four, closer to six-five, and he filled the doorway. Behind her Madelyn heard Christine gasp, but Reese didn't even glance at her; he kept his eyes on Madelyn. "Are you ready?"

"Yes," she whispered. "I'm completely packed."

"I'll put your suitcases in the car."

He was wearing a charcoal pin-striped suit with a spotlessly white shirt. Madelyn recognized both the cut and fabric as being expensive, and knew this must be a suit he'd had before his divorce. He was breathtaking in it. She glanced at Christine, who still wasn't breathing.

"Christine, this is Reese Duncan. Reese, my best friend, Christine Rizzotto."

Reese gave Christine a half smile and touched his fingers to the brim of his hat. "I'm pleased to meet you, ma'am."

She was still ogling him, but she managed a weak, "And you, Mr. Duncan."

He picked up two of Madelyn's suitcases, nodded to Christine, and carried them out. Christine's breath escaped her with a whoosh. "That man is . . . is potent," she half gasped. "Now I understand."

Madelyn knew how she felt, and fingered the string of pearls around her neck. The nervousness was coming back.

Robert's pale eyes were cool when he was introduced to Reese, which bothered Reese not at all. They were polite to each other. Madelyn hadn't hoped for anything more. Their personalities were both too strong to allow for easy companionship.

It wasn't until everyone had checked out that she realized what he had said and turned to him in bewilderment. "You said you'd put the suitcases in the car. You don't have a car."

"I do now. You'll need something to drive when I have the truck out on the range. It isn't new, but it's dependable."

She was overwhelmed, and her throat tightened. It was a white Ford station wagon, a useful vehicle on a working ranch. She'd had a car while she'd been in college in Virginia, but that had been years ago, and she hadn't had any need for one in the city. With money so tight for Reese, this was a big gesture for him to make. If she had thought about it she would have bought her own car, but she hadn't.

The judge was waiting for them in his chambers. Madelyn opened her purse and got out the ring she'd bought for Reese, slipping it on her finger and closing her hand into a fist to keep it on. The judge saw her do it, and smiled. Christine took her purse from her, and after clearing his throat twice, the judge began.

Her hands were cold. Reese held her left one, folding his hard, warm fingers over hers to share his body heat with her, and when he felt her shaking he put his arm around her waist. He repeated the vows, his dark-textured voice steady. She learned that Gideon was his first name, something she hadn't known before and hadn't gotten around to asking. When it was her turn, she was surprised to hear her own vows repeated just as evenly. He slipped a plain gold band on her finger, and the judge smoothly continued, having seen Madelyn take out Reese's ring. Reese started with surprise when the judge did the ring ceremony again, and Madelyn slid a gold band over his knuckle. It was a plain band, like hers, but he hadn't expected a ring. He hadn't worn one before. The wedding band looked odd on his hand, a thin ring of gold signaling that he was now a married man.

Then he kissed her. It was just a light touch of the lips, lingering only a moment, because he didn't want to start kissing her now. He was under control, and he wanted it to stay that way. It was done. They were married.

Madelyn was quiet as they drove Robert and Christine back to the airport. Their flight was already being called, so they didn't have time to do more than hug her fiercely. Reese shook Robert's hand, and a very male look passed between the two men. Madelyn blinked back tears as both Christine and Robert turned back to wave just before they disappeared from view.

They were alone. Reese kept his arm clamped around her waist as they walked back to the car. "You look like you're about to collapse," he growled.

She felt light-headed. "I may. I've never been married before. It's a nerve-racking business."

He put her in the car. "Have you had anything to eat today?"

She shook her head.

He was cursing when he slid under the steering wheel. "No wonder you're so shaky. We'll stop and get something."

"Not just yet, please. We can stop closer to home. I'm still too nervous right now to eat anything."

In the end, they wound up driving straight to the ranch. Reese carried her suitcases up to his bedroom. "There's a big walk-in closet," he said, opening the door to show her the enormous closet, as big as a small room. "But don't start unpacking now. You need to eat first."

She gestured to her clothes. "I'll have to change before I start cooking."

"I'll do the cooking," he said sharply.

There wasn't much cooking to it, just soup and sandwiches. Madelyn forced herself to eat half a sandwich and a bowl of soup. It all seemed so unreal. She was married. This was her home now.

Reese went upstairs and changed into his work clothes. Wedding day or no, the chores had to be done. Madelyn cleaned up the kitchen, then went upstairs and began hanging up her new clothes. His bedroom was much larger than the one she had slept in before, with a big private bath that included both bathtub and shower. The bed was king-size. She thought of lying in that bed with him and felt herself get dizzy. It was already late afternoon.

She was in the kitchen again, dressed more appropriately this time in jeans and a short-sleeved sweater, when he came in tired and dirty. "Are you hungry again?" she asked. "I can do something fast while you're showering."

"Just more sandwiches tonight," he said. "I'm not much interested in food right now." He was unbuttoning his shirt as he went up the stairs.

She made the sandwiches and sat at the table with him, drinking a glass of milk while he ate. She had never thought about how much a hard-working man needed to eat, but she could see she would have to cook twice the amount she had imagined.

"I have some paperwork to do," he said when he'd finished and carried his plate to the sink. "It won't take me long."

She understood. After she'd washed the few dishes, she went upstairs and took a bath. She had just left the bathroom, her skin flushed from the damp heat, when he entered the bedroom.

She stopped, biting her lip at the searing look he gave her from her tumbled hair down to her bare toes, as if he could see through her white cotton gown. He sat down on the bed and took off his boots, then stood and tugged his shirt free. His eyes never left her as he unbuttoned the shirt and took it off.

His chest was tanned and muscled and covered with curly black hair. The smooth skin of his shoulders gleamed as he unbuckled his belt and began unfastening his jeans.

Madelyn drew a deep breath and lifted her head. "There's something you need to know."

He paused, his eyes narrowing. She was standing ramrod straight, her pale hair swirling around her shoulders and down her back. That loose, sleeveless gown wasn't anything like the sheer silk confection April had worn, but Madelyn didn't need silk to be seductive. The shadow of her nipples pressing against the white cotton was seduction enough. What could she have to tell him that was keeping her strung as tight as fence wire?

He said softly, "Don't tell me you've decided to wait another couple of nights, because I'm not going for it. Why are you so nervous?"

She gestured at the bed. "I've never done this before."

He couldn't have heard right. Stunned, he released his zipper. "You've never had sex before?"

"No, and to be honest, I'm not really looking forward to it. I want you and I want to be intimate with you, but I don't expect to enjoy the first time." Her gaze was very direct.

An odd kind of anger shook him. "Damn it, Maddie, if you're a virgin why didn't you say so, instead of having that damn physical?"

She looked like a haughty queen. "For one thing, we weren't married before. Until you became my husband this morning it wasn't any of your business. For another, you wouldn't have believed me. You believe me now because there's no reason for me to lie when you'll find out the truth for yourself in a few minutes." She spoke with cool dignity, her head high.

"We were planning to get married."

"And it could have been called off."

Reese stared silently at her. Part of him was stunned and elated. No other man had ever had her; she was completely his. He was selfish enough, male enough, primitive enough, to be glad the penetration of her maidenhead would be his right. But part of him was disappointed, because this ruled out the night of hungry lovemaking he'd planned; he would have to be a total bastard to be that insensitive to her. She would be too sore and tender for extended loving.

Maybe this was for the best. He'd take her as gently as possible, but he wouldn't, couldn't, lose his control with her. He wouldn't let himself drown in her; he would simply consummate the marriage as swiftly and easily as he could and preserve the distance between them. He didn't want to give in completely to the fierce desire in him, he just wanted to ease himself and keep her in the slot he'd assigned to her. He wanted her too much; she was a threat to him in every way he'd sworn a woman would never be again. As long as he could keep his passion for her under control she wouldn't be able to breach his defenses, so he would allow himself only a simple mating. He wouldn't linger over her, feast on her, as he wanted to do.

Madelyn forced herself not to tremble when he walked over to her. It had been nothing less than the bald truth when she'd said she wasn't looking forward to this first time. Romantically, she wanted a night of rapture. Realistically, she expected much less. All they had shared was one kiss, and Reese was sexually frustrated, his control stretched to the limit. She was going to open her body to a stranger, and she couldn't help being apprehensive.

He saw the almost imperceptible way she braced herself as he came near, and he slid his hand into her hair. "You don't have to be afraid," he murmured. "I'm not going to jump on you like a bull." He tilted her head up so she had to look at him. His eyes were greener than she'd ever seen them before. "I can make it good for you, baby."

She swallowed. "I'd rather you didn't try, I think, not this time. I'm too nervous, and it might not work, and then I'd be disappointed. Just do it and get it over with."

A faint smile touched his lips. "That's the last thing a woman should ever say to a man." It was also a measure of her fear. "The slower I am, the better it will be for you."

"Unless I have a nervous breakdown in the middle of it."

She wasn't joking. He rubbed his thumb over her bottom lip, feeling the softness of it. It was beginning to make sense. A woman who reached the age of twenty-eight still a virgin had to have a strong sense of reserve about being intimate with a man. The way she'd kissed him had set him on fire, but this final step wasn't one she took easily. She preferred to gradually get used to this powerful new intimacy, rather than throw herself totally into the experience expecting stars and fireworks.

He picked her up and put her on the bed, then turned out all the lights except for one lamp. Madelyn would have preferred total darkness but didn't say anything. She couldn't stop staring when he stripped off his jeans and got into bed with her. She had seen male nudity before: babies and little boys, men in clinical magazines. She knew how the male body functioned. But she had never before seen a fully aroused man, and Reese was definitely that. She lost her hope for nothing worse than discomfort.

He was a big man. He leaned over her, and she felt totally dwarfed by the width of his chest and shoulders, the muscled power of his body. She could barely breathe, her lungs pumping desperately for quick, shallow gasps. By her own will and actions she had brought herself to this, placed herself in bed with a man she didn't know.

He slid his hand under her nightgown and up her thigh, his hard, warm palm shocking on her bare skin. The nightgown was pulled upward by his action, steadily baring more and more of her body until the gown was around her waist and she lay exposed to him. She closed her eyes tightly, wondering if she could go through with this.

He pulled the nightgown completely off. She shivered as she felt him against every inch of her bare body. "It won't be horrible," he murmured as he brushed her lips in a gentle kiss. "I'll make certain of it." Then she felt him close his mouth on her nipple, and the incredible heat and pressure made her moan. She kept her eyes closed as he stroked and fondled her body until gradually the tension eased and she was pliable under his hands.

Her senses couldn't reach fever pitch. She was too tired and nervous. He slid his hand between her legs and she jumped, her body tensing again even though she parted her thighs and allowed him the intimacy. His long fingers gently parted and stroked, probed to find both the degree of her readiness and the strength of her virginity. When his finger slid into her she flinched and turned her head against his shoulder.

"Shh, it's all right," he murmured soothingly. He stretched to reach the bedside table and opened the top drawer to retrieve the tube of lubricant he had put in there earlier. She flinched again at the cool slickness of it as his finger entered her once more and moved gently back and forth.

Her heart was slamming so hard against her ribs that she thought she might be sick. He mounted her, his muscled thighs spreading hers wide, and her eyes flew open in quick panic. She subdued the fear, forcing herself to relax as much as possible. "I'm sorry," she whispered. "I know you wanted it to be better than this."

He rubbed his lips over hers, and she clung to him, her nails digging into his shoulders as she felt his hips lift and his hardness begin to probe her. "I wish it were better for you," he said in a low, taut voice. "But I'm glad you're a virgin, that this first time is mine." Then he started entering her.

She couldn't prevent the tears that scalded her eyes and ran down her temples. He was as gentle as possible, but she didn't accept him easily. The stretching and penetration of her body was a burning pain, and the rhythmic motions of his body only added to it. The only thing that made it bearable for her was, perversely, the very intimacy of having her body so deeply invaded by the man she loved. She was shattered by how primitively natural it was to give herself to him and let him find pleasure within her. Beyond the pain was a growing warmth that promised much more.

5

The alarm went off at four-thirty. She felt him stretch beside her and reach out to shut off the insistent buzzing. Then he sat up, yawning, and turned on the lamp. She blinked at the sudden bright light.

Unconcernedly naked, he went into the bathroom. Madelyn used the privacy to bound out of bed and scramble into her clothes. She was just stepping into her jeans when he came out to begin dressing. His eyes lingered on her legs as she pulled the jeans up and snapped them.

Surrounded by the early-morning quiet and darkness, with only the one lamp lighting the room, looking at his naked body seemed as intimate as the night before when he had entered her. Warmth surged in her as she realized that intimacy had many facets. It wasn't just sex, it was being at ease with each other, the daily routine of nakedness and dressing together.

As he dressed, he watched her drag a brush through her hair in several swift strokes, restoring it to casual order. Her slender body bent and swayed with a feminine grace that made it impossible for him to look away. He remembered the way it had felt to be inside her the night before, the tightness and heat, and against his will his loins responded. He couldn't take her now; she would be too tender. She had cried the night before, and every tear had burned him. He could wait.

She put the brush down and began plumping the pillows. He went over to help her make the bed, but when she threw the tumbled covers back to straighten the bottom sheet, she saw the red stains smeared on the linen and went still.

Reese looked at the stains, too, wondering if she had any pleasure to remember as he had, or if they reminded her only of the pain. He bent and tugged the sheet loose and began stripping the bed. "The next time will be better," he said, and she gave him such a solemn look that he wanted to hold her in his arms and rock her. If she had wanted it, he could have brought her to pleasure in other ways, but she had made it plain she wasn't ready for that. He wondered how he would be able to retain his control if she did give him the total freedom of her body. That one, restricted episode of lovemaking hadn't come close to satisfying the surging hunger he felt, and that was the danger of it.

He tossed the sheet to the floor. "I'll do the morning chores while you cook breakfast."

Madelyn nodded. As he went out the door she called, "Wait! Do you like pancakes?"

He paused and looked back. "Yes, and a lot of them."

She remembered from her earlier visit that he liked his coffee strong. She yawned as she went downstairs to the kitchen; then she stood in the middle of the room and looked around. It was difficult to know where to begin when you didn't know where anything was.

Coffee first. At least his coffee maker was an automatic drip. She found the filters and dipped in enough coffee to make the brew twice as strong as she would have made it for herself.

She had to guess at the amount of bacon and sausage to fry. As hard as he worked, he would need an enormous amount of food to eat, since he would normally burn off four or five thousand calories a day. As the combined smells of brewing coffee and frying breakfast meats began to fill the kitchen, she realized for the first time what an ongoing chore just the cooking would be. She would have to become very familiar with some cookbooks, because her skills tended toward the most basic.

Thank God he had pancake mix. She stirred up the batter, searched out the syrup, then set the table. How long should she give him before she poured the pancakes on the griddle?

A heaping platter of bacon and sausage was browned and on the table before he came back from the barn, carrying a pail of fresh milk. As soon as the door opened, Madelyn poured four circles of batter on the griddle. He put the milk on the countertop and turned on the tap to wash his hands. "How much longer will it be until breakfast is ready?"

"Two minutes. Pancakes don't take long." She flipped them over. "The coffee's ready."

He poured himself a cup and leaned against the cabinet beside her, watching her stand guard over the pancakes. It was only a couple of minutes before she stacked them on a plate and handed it to him. "The butter's on the table. Start on these while I cook some more."

He carried the plate to the table and began eating. He was finished with the first round of pancakes by the time the second was ready. Madelyn poured four more circles on the griddle. This made an even dozen. How many would he eat?

He only ate ten. She got the remaining two from the last batch and slid onto a chair beside him. "What are you doing today?"

"I have to check fences in the west quarter so I can move the herd there for grazing."

"Will you be back for lunch, or should I pack some sandwiches?"

"Sandwiches."

And that, she thought half an hour later when he'd saddled a horse and ridden out, was that. So much for conversation over breakfast. He hadn't even kissed her this morning. She knew he had a lot of work to do, but a pat on the head wouldn't have taken too much of his time.

Their first full day of marriage didn't appear to be starting out too well.

Then she wondered just what she had expected. She knew how Reese felt, knew he didn't want her to get too close to him. It would take time to break down those barriers. The best thing she could do was learn how to be a rancher's wife. She didn't have time to fret because he hadn't kissed her good morning.

She cleaned the kitchen, which became an entire morning's work. She mopped the floor, scrubbed the oven, cleaned out the big double refrigerator, and re-arranged the pantry so she'd know where everything was. She inventoried the pantry and started a list of things she'd need. She did the laundry and remade the bed with fresh linens. She vacuumed and dusted both upstairs and down, cleaned the three bathrooms, sewed buttons on his shirts and repaired a myriad of small rips in his shirts and jeans. All in all, she felt very domestic.

Marriage was work, after all. It wasn't an endless round of parties and romantic picnics by a river.

Marriage was also night after night in bed with the same man, opening her arms and thighs to him, easing his passion within her. He'd said it would be better, and she sensed that it would, that she had just been too tired and tense the night before for it to have been pleasurable no matter what he'd done. The whole process had been a bit shocking. No matter how much she had technically known about sex, nothing had prepared her for the reality of penetration, of actually feeling his hardness inside her. Her heartbeat picked up speed as she thought of the coming night.

She started unpacking some of the boxes she had shipped, reassembling the stereo equipment and putting some of her books out. She was so busy that when she noted the time, it was almost dark. Reese would be coming in soon, and she hadn't even started dinner. She stopped what she was doing and raced to the kitchen. She hadn't even planned what they would have, but at least she knew what was in the pantry.

A quick check of the freezer produced some thick steaks and one pack of pork chops and very little else. She made mental additions to the grocery list as she unwrapped the chops and put them in the microwave to defrost. If he hadn't had a microwave she would have been in big trouble. She was peeling a small mountain of potatoes when the back door opened. She heard him scrape his boots, then sigh tiredly as he took them off.

He came into the kitchen and stopped, looking around at the bare table and stove. "Why isn't dinner ready?" he asked in a very quiet, ominous tone.

"I was busy and didn't notice the time—"

"It's your job to notice the time. I'm dead tired and hungry. I've worked twelve hours straight, the least you could do is take the time to cook."

His words stung, but she didn't pause in what she was doing. "I'm doing it as fast as I can. Go take a shower and relax for a few minutes."

He stomped up the stairs. She bit her lip as she cut up the potatoes and put them in a pan of hot water to stew. If he hadn't looked so exhausted she might have told him a few things, but he'd been slumping with weariness and filthy from head to foot. His day hadn't been an easy one.

She opened a big can of green beans and dumped it into a pan, then added seasonings. The chops were already baking. Bread. She needed bread. There were no canned biscuits in the refrigerator. She couldn't dredge the recipe for biscuits from her memory, no matter how many times she'd watched Grandma Lily make them. She found the cookbooks and began checking the indexes for biscuits.

Once she had the list of ingredients before her it all began to come back. She mixed the dough, then kneaded it and rolled it out as she'd done when she was a little girl. She couldn't find a biscuit cutter, so she used a water glass, pressing it down into the dough and coming up with a perfect circle. A few minutes later, a dozen biscuits were popped into the oven.

Dessert. She'd seen some small, individually wrapped devil's food cakes. She got those out, and a big can of peaches. It would have to do, because she didn't have time to bake. She opened the can of peaches and poured them into a bowl.

By the time she had the table set, Reese had come back downstairs, considerably cleaner but unimproved in mood. He looked pointedly at the empty table and stalked into the living room.

She checked the potatoes; they were tender. She mixed up a small amount of flour and milk and poured it into the potatoes; it instantly began thickening. She let them stew while she checked the chops and green beans.

The biscuits were golden brown, and had risen nicely. Now if only they were edible... Since she'd followed a recipe, they shouldn't be too bad, she hoped. She stacked them on a plate and crossed her fingers for luck.

The chops were done, finally. "Reese! Dinner's ready."

"It's about time."

She hurried to put the food on the table, realizing at the last minute that she had made neither coffee nor tea. Quickly she got two glasses from the cabinet and poured milk. She knew that he liked milk, so perhaps he sometimes drank it at dinner.

The chops weren't the tenderest she'd ever cooked, and the biscuits were a bit heavy, but he ate steadily, without comment. Heavy or not, the dozen biscuits disappeared in short order, and she ate only one. As his third helping of stewed potatoes was disappearing, she got up. "Do you want any dessert?"

His head came up. "Dessert?"

She couldn't help smiling. You could tell the man had lived alone for seven years. "It isn't much, because I didn't get around to baking." She put the small cakes in a bowl and dipped peaches and juice over them. Reese gave them a quizzical look as she set the bowl in front of him.

"Just try it," she said. "I know it's junk food, but it tastes good."

He did, and cleaned the bowl. Some of the fatigue was fading from his face. "The stereo in the living room looks like a good one."

"I've had it for several years. I hope it survived the shipping."

He'd sold his stereo system years ago, deciding that he needed the money more than he needed the music, and he'd never let himself think too much about it. When you were fighting for survival, you quickly learned how to get your priorities in order. But he'd missed music and was looking forward to playing some of his old classics again.

The house was full of signs of what she'd been doing all day, and he felt guilty about yelling at her because dinner hadn't been ready. The floors were cleaner than they'd been in years, and the dust was gone from every surface. The house smelled of household cleaner and furniture polish, and the bathroom had sparkled with cleanliness. The house was ten rooms and over four thousand square feet; his fancy city woman knew how to work.

He helped her clean the table and load the dishwasher. "What's that?" he asked, pointing to her list.

"The shopping list. The pantry has a limited selection."

He shrugged. "I was usually so tired I just ate sandwiches."

"How far is the nearest market? And don't tell me I'm going to have to go to Billings."

"There's a general store about twenty miles from here. It isn't a supermarket, but you can get the basics there. I'll take you there day after tomorrow. I can't do it tomorrow because I've got more fencing to repair before I can move the herd."

"Just give me directions. I don't think the food situation will wait until the day after tomorrow."

"I don't want you out wandering around," he said flatly.

"I won't be wandering. Just give me the directions."

"I'd rather you wait. I don't know how reliable the car is yet."

"Then I can take the truck."

"I said I'll take you day after tomorrow, and that's that."

Fuming, she went upstairs and took a shower. Why on earth was he so intractable? The way he'd acted, she might as well have said she was going to find a bar and spend the day in it. But then, that might have been what his first wife had done. Even if it were true, Madelyn was determined that she wasn't going to spend her life paying for April's sins.

She finished unpacking her clothes, hanging most of her New York clothes in the closet in another bedroom, since she wouldn't have much use for them now. It still made her feel strange to see her clothes in the same closet with a man's; she'd shared room, closet and clothes in college, but that was different. This was serious. This was a lifetime.

One thing about getting up at four-thirty: she was already sleepy, and it was only eight. Of course, she was still feeling the effects of not getting enough sleep for the past two weeks, as well as a very active day, but she could barely hold her eyes open.

She heard Reese come upstairs and go into their bedroom; then he called, ''Maddie?'' in a rougher voice than usual.

''In here,'' she called.

He appeared in the doorway, and his eyes sharpened as he took in the clothes piled on the bed. ''What're you doing?'' There was an oddly tense set to his shoulders.

''I'm hanging the clothes I won't use in here, so they won't clutter up our closet.''

Maybe it was only her imagination, but he appeared to relax. ''Are you ready to go to bed?''

''Yes, I can finish this tomorrow.''

He stood aside to let her get past him, then turned out the light and followed her down the hall. Madelyn was barefoot and in another thin gown much like the one she'd worn the night before, and she got that dwarfed, suffocated feeling again, sensing him so close behind her. The top of her head would just reach his chin, and he had to weigh at least two hundred pounds, all of it muscle. It would be easy to let herself be intimidated by him, especially when she thought of lying beneath him on that big bed. She would be going to bed with him like this for the rest of her life. Maybe he had doubts about the longevity of their marriage, but she didn't.

It was easier this time. She lay in his muscular arms and felt the warmth grow under his stroking hands. But now that she was less nervous she sensed something wrong, as if he were keeping part of himself separate from their lovemaking. He touched her, but only under strict control, as if he were allowing himself only so much enjoyment and not a bit more. She didn't want those measured touches, she wanted his passion. She knew it was there, she sensed it, but he wasn't giving it to her.

It still hurt when he entered her, though not as much as before. He was gentle, but he wasn't loving. This was the way he would have treated either of those other two women he'd been willing to marry, she thought dimly, as a body he'd been given the use of, not as a warm, loving woman who needed more. This was only sex, not making love. He made her feel like a faceless stranger.

This was war. As she went to sleep afterward, she was planning her campaign.

"I want to go with you today," she said the next morning over breakfast.

He didn't look up from his eggs and biscuits. "You're not up to it."

"How do you know?" she retorted.

He looked annoyed. "Because a lot of *men* aren't up to it."

"You're repairing fencing today, right? I can help you with the wire and at least keep you company."

That was exactly what Reese didn't want. If he spent a lot of time in her company he'd end up making love to her, and that was something he wanted to limit. If he could hold himself to once a night, he'd be able to keep everything under control.

"It'll only take a couple of hours to finish repairing the fence, then I'll bring the truck home and go back out on horseback to move the herd."

"I told you, I can ride."

He shook his head impatiently. "How long has it been since you've been on a horse? What kind of riding did you do, tame trail riding on a rented hack? This is open country, and my horses are trained to work cattle."

"Granted, it's been almost a year since I've been on a horse, but I know all about liniment. I have to get used to it sometime."

"You'd just be in the way. Stay here and see if you can have dinner done on time tonight."

She narrowed her eyes and put her hands on her hips. "Reese Duncan, I'm going with you and that's final."

He got up from the table. "You'd better learn that this is my ranch, and what I say goes. That includes you. A few words by a judge doesn't give you any say-so in my work. I do the ranch work, you take care of the house. I want fried chicken for dinner, so you can get started on that."

"There isn't any chicken in the freezer," she retorted. "Since you don't want me to go shopping, I guess you'll have to change your request."

He pointed out to the yard. "There are plenty of chickens out there, city slicker. Meat doesn't always come shrink-wrapped."

Madelyn's temper was usually as languorous as her walk, but she'd had enough. "You want me to catch a chicken?" she asked, tight-lipped. "You don't think I can do it, do you? That's why you said it. You want to show me how much I don't know about ranch life. You'll have your damn chicken for dinner, if I have to ram it down your throat feathers and all!"

She turned and stormed up the stairs. Reese stood there, a little taken aback. He hadn't known Madelyn could move that fast.

She was back downstairs before he could get the truck loaded and leave. He heard the back door slam and turned. His eyes widened. She had strapped protective pads on her knees and elbows, with the knee-pads over her jeans. She'd put on athletic shoes. She still looked furious, and she didn't even glance at him. Reese hooked his thumbs in his belt loops and leaned against the truck to watch.

She picked out a hen and eased up to it, scattering a few handfuls of feed to lure the birds. Reese lifted his eyebrows, impressed. But she made her move just a little too soon; the hen squawked and ran for her life with Madelyn in pursuit.

She dove for the bird, sliding along the ground on her belly and just missing the frantic bird. Reese winced and straightened away from the truck, horrified at the thought of what the dirt and rocks were doing to her soft skin, but she jumped up and took off after the hen. The bird ran in erratic circles around the yard, then darted under the truck. Madelyn swerved

to head it off, and another headlong tackle fell an inch
short.

"Look, just forget about the chick—" he began,
but she was already gone.

The bird managed to take flight enough to land in
the lower branches of a tree, but it was still over Madelyn's head. She narrowed her eyes and bent to pick a
few rocks up from the ground. She wound up and let
fly. The rock went over the chicken's head. The hen
pulled her head down, her bright little eyes glittering. The next rock hit the limb next to her and she
squawked, shifing position. The third rock hit her on
the leg, and she took flight again.

This time Madelyn judged her dive perfectly. She
slid along the ground in a flurry of dust and pebbles,
and her hand closed over one of the hen's legs. The
bird immediately went wild, flapping her wings and
trying to peck the imprisoning hand that held her.
They grappled in the dust for a minute, but then Madelyn stood up with the hen upside down and firmly
held by both feet, its wings spread. Her hands were
dotted with blood where the furious hen had pecked
her, breaking the skin. "Faster than a speeding pul-
let," she said with grim triumph.

Reese could only stare at her in silence as she stalked
up to him. Her hair was a mess, tangled and hanging
in her eyes. Her face was caked with dust, her shirt was
filthy and torn, and her jeans were a mess. One kneepad had come loose and was drooping down her shin.
The look in those gray eyes, however, kept him from
laughing. He didn't dare even smile.

The chicken hit him in the chest, and he grabbed for it, just preventing the bird from making a break for freedom.

"There's your damn chicken," she said between her teeth. "I hope you're very happy together." She slammed back into the house.

Reese looked down at the bird and remembered the blood on Madelyn's hands. He wrung the hen's neck with one quick, competent twist. He'd never felt less like laughing.

He carried the dead bird inside and dropped it on the floor. Madelyn was standing at the sink, carefully soaping her hands. "Let me see," he said, coming up behind her and reaching around to take her hands in his, effectively pinning her in place. The hen had drawn blood in several places, painful little puncture wounds that were blue around the edges. He'd had a few of them himself and knew how easily they could become infected.

He reached for a towel to wrap around her hands. "Come upstairs to the bathroom and I'll put disinfectant on them."

She didn't move. "It's my hands, not my back. I can reach them just fine, thank you. I'll do it myself."

His muscled arms were iron bands around her; his hard hands held her easily. Her front was pressed against the sink, and his big body was against her back, hemming her in, holding her. She felt utterly surrounded by him and had the sudden violent thought that she should never have married someone who was almost a foot taller than she was. She was at a woeful disadvantage here.

He bent, hooked his right arm under her knees and lifted her with insulting ease. Madelyn grabbed for his shoulders to keep her balance. "The hen pecked my hands, not my feet," she said caustically.

He slanted a warning look at her as he started up the stairs.

"Men who use force against women are lower than slugs."

His arms tightened, but he kept a tight rein on his temper. He carried her into the bathroom and put her on her feet. As he opened the medicine cabinet she headed out the door, and he grabbed her with one hand, hauling her back. She tugged violently, trying to free her arm. "I said I'd do it myself!" she said, furious with him.

He put the lid down on the toilet, sat down and pulled her onto his lap. "Be still and let me clean your hands. If you still want to fight after I'm finished, then I'll be glad to oblige you."

Fuming, Madelyn sat on his lap while he dabbed the small wounds with an antiseptic that stung sharply. Then he smoothed antibiotic cream on them and put Band-Aids over the two worst breaks. His arms were still around her; he was holding her as a parent would a child, to soothe it and tend its hurts. She didn't like the comparison, even if it was her own. She shifted restlessly, feeling his hard thighs under her bottom.

His face was very close to hers. She could see all the different colored specks in his eyes, green and blue dominating, but shot through with black and white and a few glittering flecks of gold. Though he had shaved the night before, his beard had already grown enough to roughen his cheeks and chin. The brackets on each side of his mouth framed the beautiful cut of his lips, and suddenly she remembered the way he had closed those lips over her nipple, sucking her tender flesh into his mouth. She quivered, and the rigidity went out of her body.

Reese closed the first-aid box and set it aside, then let his arm rest loosely across her thighs as he gave her a measuring look. "Your face is dirty."

"So let me up and I'll wash it."

He didn't. He washed it himself, slowly drawing a wet washcloth over her features, the fabric almost caressing her skin. He wiped her mouth with a touch so light she could barely feel it and watched the cloth tug slightly at her soft, enticing lower lip. Madelyn's head tilted back, and her eyelids drooped. He drew the cloth down her neck, wiped it across her exposed collarbone, then dipped his hand down inside the loose neck of her top.

She caught her breath at the damp coolness on her breasts. He drew the cloth back and forth, slowly rasping it across her nipples and bringing them to wet attention. Her breasts began to throb, and her back arched involuntarily, offering them for more. She could feel a hard ridge growing, pressing against her hip, and her blood moved heavily through her veins.

He tossed the washcloth into the basin and took his hat off, dropping it onto the floor. The arm behind her back tightened and drew her in to him as he bent his head, and his mouth closed over hers.

It was the same way he'd kissed her in the airport, the way he hadn't kissed her since. His mouth was hard and hot, urgent in his demands. His tongue pushed into her mouth, and she met it with her own, welcoming, enticing, wanting more.

She gave way beneath his onslaught, her head falling back against his shoulder. He pursued the advantage, taking her mouth again, putting his hand beneath her shirt and closing it over her breast. Gently he kneaded the firm mound, rubbing his rough palm over the nipple until she whimpered into his mouth from the exquisite pain of it. She turned toward him, lifting her arms around his neck. Excitement pounded in the pit of her stomach, tightening every muscle in her body and starting an aching tension between her legs.

With a rough sound of passion he bent her back over his arm and shoved her top up, exposing her breasts. His warm breath feathered across them as he bent to her; then he extended the tip of his tongue and circled one pink nipple, making it constrict into a tightly puckered nub and turn reddish. He shifted her body, bringing her other breast closer to his mouth, and gave that nipple identical treatment, watching with pleasure as it, too, tightened.

Madelyn clutched at him. "Reese," she begged in a low, shaking voice. She needed him.

This was the hot magic she had sensed about him from the beginning, the blatant sensuality. This was the warm promise she had felt lying beneath him at night, and she wanted more.

He drew her nipple into his mouth with a strong, sucking pressure, and she arched again, her thighs shifting. She felt like a dessert offered up to him, lying across his lap with her body lifted to his mouth, glorying in the way his lips and teeth and tongue worked at her breast.

"Reese," she said again. It was little more than a moan, heavy with desire. Everything that was male in him responded to that female cry of need, urging him to surge deep within her and ease the empty ache that made her twist in his arms and cry out for him. His loins were throbbing, his body radiating heat. If she needed to be filled, he needed to fill her. The two restrained matings he'd had with her hadn't been enough, would never satisfy the lust that intensified every time he looked at her.

But if he ever let himself go with her, he'd never be able to get that control back. April had taught him a bitter lesson, one that he relearned every day when he worked on his diminished acres, or saw the paint peeling on his house. Madelyn might never turn on him, but he couldn't take the chance and let his guard down.

With an effort that brought sweat to his brow, he lifted his mouth from her maddeningly sweet flesh and shifted her to her feet. She swayed, her eyes dazed, her top twisted up under her arms and exposing those firm, round breasts. She didn't understand and reached for him, offering a drugging sensuality that he wouldn't let himself take.

He caught her wrists and held her arms to her sides while he stood up, an action that brought their bodies together. He heard her moan softly again, and she let her head fall forward against his chest, where she rubbed her cheek back and forth in a subtle caress that made him curse his shirt for covering his bare skin.

If he didn't get out of here now, he wouldn't go at all.

"I have work to do." His voice was hoarse with strain. She didn't move. She was melting against him, her slim hips starting a drumbeat roll that rocked into his loins and made him feel as if his pants would split under the pressure.

"Madelyn, stop it. I have to go."

"Yes," she whispered, rising on tiptoe to brush her lips against his throat.

His hands closed tightly on her hips, for one convulsive second pulling her into his pelvis as if he would grind himself into her; then he pushed her away. He picked up his hat and strode from the bathroom before she could recover and reach for him again, because he damn sure wouldn't have the strength to stop this time.

Madelyn stared after him, confused by his sudden departure and aching from the loss of contact. She swayed; then realization burst within her, and she gave a hoarse cry of mingled rage and pain, putting her hand out to catch the basin so she wouldn't fall to her knees.

Damn him, damn him, damn him! He'd brought her to fever pitch, then left her empty and aching. She knew he'd wanted her; she had felt his hardness, felt the tension in his corded muscles. He could have carried her to the bed or even had her right there in the bathroom, and she would have gloried in it, but instead he'd pushed her away.

He'd been too close to losing control. Like a flash she knew what had happened, knew that at the last minute he'd had to prove to himself that he could still walk away from her, that he didn't want her so much that he couldn't master it. The sexuality of his nature was so strong that it kept burning through those walls he'd built around himself, but he was still fighting it, and so far he'd won.

Slowly she went downstairs, holding the banister because her knees felt like overcooked noodles. If she were to have any chance with him at all, she would have to find some way to shatter that iron control, but she didn't know if her nerves or self-esteem would hold out.

He was already gone, the truck nowhere in sight. She looked around blankly, unable to think what she should do, and her eyes lit on the dead chicken lying on the floor.

"I'll get back at you for this," she said with grim promise in her voice, and began the loathsome task of getting that blasted hen ready to cook.

6

When Reese came in that evening, Madelyn didn't look up from the bowl of potatoes she was mashing. The force with which she wielded the potato masher went far beyond what was required and carried a hint of savagery. One look at her averted face told Reese she was probably imagining using that potato masher on him. He looked thoughtful. He'd expected her to be cool, maybe even a little hurt, but he hadn't expected her temper to still be at boiling point; it took a lot of energy to sustain a rage that many hours. Evidently it took her as long to cool off as it did to lose her temper to begin with.

He said, "It'll take me about fifteen minutes to get cleaned up."

She still didn't look up. "Dinner will be ready in ten."

From that he deduced that she wasn't going to wait for him. The thoughtful look deepened as he went upstairs.

He took one of the fastest showers of his life and thought about not shaving, but he didn't like the idea of scraping her soft skin with his beard, so he ran the risk of cutting his own throat due to the speed with which he dragged the razor across his skin. He was

barefoot and still buttoning his shirt when he went
back down the stairs.

She was just placing the glasses of iced tea on the
table, and they sat down together. The platter of fried
chicken was sitting right in front of his plate. He'd either have to eat the damn bird or wear it, he decided.

He piled his plate with chicken, mashed potatoes,
biscuits and gravy, all the while eying the platter curi-
ously. He continued to examine the contents while he
took his first bite and controlled a grunt of pleasure.
The chicken was tender, the crust crisp and spicy.
Madelyn made a better cook than he'd expected. But
the remaining pieces of chicken looked . . . strange.

"What piece is that?" he asked, pointing at a
strangely configured section of chicken.

"I have no idea," she replied without looking at
him. "I've never cleaned and butchered my food before."

He bit the inside of his cheek to keep from grinning. If he made the mistake of laughing she would
probably dump the bowl of gravy over his head.

The meal was strained and mostly silent. If he made
a comment, she replied, but other than that she made
no effort to hold a conversation. She ate a small portion of each item, though minuscule was perhaps a
better word. As soon as she was finished she carried
her plate to the sink and brought back a clean saucer,
as well as a cherry cobbler that was still bubbling.

Very little in life had ever interfered with Reese's
appetite, and tonight was no exception. He worked too
hard to pick at his food. By the time Madelyn had
finished dabbling with a small helping of cobbler he
had demolished most of the chicken, all the potatoes

and gravy, and only two biscuits were left. He was feeling almost contented as Madelyn placed an enormous portion of cobbler onto a clean plate for him. A quick look at her icy face, however, told him that food hadn't worked the same miracle on her.

"How did you learn to cook like this?"

"There are cookbooks in the cabinet. I can read."

So much for that conversational gambit.

She went upstairs immediately after the kitchen was clean. Reese went into his office and took a stab at the paperwork that never ended, but his mind wasn't on it, and by eight o'clock he was glancing at his watch, wondering if Madelyn was ready to go to bed. He'd already heard the shower running, and the image of her standing nude under the steaming water had had him shifting restlessly in his chair. There were times when a man's sexual organs could make him damned uncomfortable, and this was one of them. He'd been hard most of the day, cursing himself for not having made love to her that morning, even though it would have been a huge mistake.

He tossed the pen onto his desk and closed the books, getting to his feet with restrained violence. Damn it, he needed her, and he couldn't wait any longer.

He turned out the lights as he went upstairs, his tread heavy and deliberate. His mind was on that searing, gut-wrenching moment when he first entered her, feeling the small resistance of her tight flesh, the giving, the enveloping, then the wet, clasping heat and his senses exploding. It was all he could do not to keep after her time and again, to try to remember that she was very new to lovemaking and still tender, to stay in control.

The bedroom door was open. He walked in and found her sitting on the bed painting her toenails, her long legs bare and curled in one of those positions that only females seemed able to achieve and males went crazy looking at. His whole body tightened, and he became fully, painfully erect. She was wearing a dark pink satin chemise that ended at the tops of her thighs and revealed matching petal pants. The satin molded to her breasts, revealing their round shape and soft nipples. Her blond hair was pulled to one side, tumbling over her shoulder, and her skin was still delicately flushed from her shower. Her expression was solemn and intent as she concentrated on the strokes of the tiny brush that turned her toenails the same deep pink as the chemise.

"Let's go to bed." His voice was guttural. He was already peeling off his shirt.

She hadn't even glanced at him. "I can't. My toenails are wet."

He didn't much care. He'd keep her legs raised long enough that the polish would be dry when he'd finished.

She capped the polish bottle and set it aside, then bent bonelessly over to blow on her toes. Reese unsnapped and unzipped his jeans. "Come to bed anyway."

She gave him an impatient look and got to her feet. "You go on. I'll go downstairs and read awhile."

He stretched his arm out in front of her when she would have passed, barring her way. His hand closed on her upper arm. "Forget reading," he muttered, pulling her toward him.

Madelyn wrenched away, staring at him in incredulous anger. "I don't believe this! You actually think I could want to make love *now*?"

His eyebrows lowered, and he hooked his thumbs in his belt loops. "Why not?" he asked very softly.

"For one very good reason. I'm angry! What you did stinks, and I'm not even close to forgiving you for it." Just the way he was standing there with his thumbs in his belt loops, his jeans open and his attitude one of incredible male arrogance, made her so angry she almost couldn't talk.

"The best way to make up is in bed."

"That's what men think," she said scornfully. "Let me tell you, no woman wants to make love with a man while she's still thinking how funny it would have been if he'd choked on a chicken bone!" She whirled and stalked barefoot from the bedroom.

Reese began swearing. Frustration boiled up in him, and for a moment he started after her. He reached the door and stopped, then slammed his fist into the door frame. Damn it all to hell!

The atmosphere was decidedly chilly between them the next morning when he drove her to the small town of Crook to buy groceries. Though she was no longer so furious, she was no less determined. He couldn't reject her one time and the next expect her to accommodate him without question. If that was his idea of what a marriage should be, they were both in for some rocky times.

To call Crook a town was to flatter it. There were a few residences sprawled out in a haphazard manner, a service station, a feed store, the general store, and a small café with the expected assortment of pickup trucks parked in front of it. Madelyn wondered just what sort of dangerous behavior Reese had expected her to get up to in Crook. Maybe he thought she'd run wild and drive on the sidewalks, which looked as if someone had already done so. They were actually wood, and were the only sidewalks she'd ever seen with skidmarks on them.

"Let's get a cup of coffee," Reese suggested as they got out of the station wagon, and Madelyn agreed. It would be nice to have a cup of coffee she didn't have to water down before she could drink it.

The café had five swivel stools, covered in split black imitation leather, in front of the counter. Three round tables were each surrounded by four chairs, and along the left side were three booths. Four of the stools were occupied, evidently by the owners of the four trucks outside. The men had different features but were identical in weathered skin, battered hats, and worn jeans and boots. Reese nodded to all of them, and they nodded back, then returned their attention to their coffee and pie.

He guided her to a booth, and they slid onto the plastic seats. The waitress behind the counter gave them a sour look. "You want something to eat, or just coffee?"

"Coffee," Reese said.

She came out from behind the counter and plunked two coffee cups down in front of them. Then she went back for the coffeepot and returned to pour the coffee, all without changing her expression, which bordered on a glare. "Coffee's fifty cents a cup," she said as if it were their fault, then marched back to her post behind the counter.

Madelyn sighed as she saw how black the coffee was. A tentative sip told her that this, too, was strong enough to strip paint.

One of the men eased down from the stool and went over to the corner jukebox. The waitress looked up. "I'll unplug that thing if you play one of them cater-wauling love songs," she said, her voice just as sour as her looks.

"You'll owe me a quarter if you do."

"And don't play none of them god-awful rock songs, neither. I don't like music where the singers sound like they're being gelded."

Madelyn's eyes rounded, and she choked a little on the coffee. Fascinated, she stared at the waitress.

The cowboy was grumbling, "I don't know of nothing you *do* like, Floris, so just shut your ears and don't listen."

"I'll tell you what I like," she snapped. "I like peace and quiet."

"Then find some library to work in." He jammed his quarter into the slot and defiantly punched buttons.

A rollicking country song filled the café. Floris began clattering cups and saucers and silverware. Madelyn wondered what the breakage bill was every month if Floris began abusing the crockery every time someone played the jukebox. The cowboy glared, and Floris banged louder. He stomped back to the jukebox and fed it another quarter, but in the manner of vending machines everywhere, it took the coin but refused his selection. He scowled and beat it with his fist. The arm scratched across the record with a hair raising screech, then, having reached the end of the groove, lifted automatically as the record was returned to its slot, and silence reigned.

With a triumphant look Floris sailed through the swinging door into the kitchen.

"The waitress from hell," Madelyn breathed in awe, watching the door swing gently back and forth.

Reese choked and had to spit his coffee back into the cup. She didn't want to look at him, but the urge was irresistible. Without turning her head she glanced toward him and found him watching her, his face unnaturally stiff. She looked at him, and he looked at her, and they began snickering. He tried to control it and quickly gulped his coffee, but Madelyn was still giggling as he grabbed for his wallet. He threw a dollar and change on the table, grabbed her hand and pulled her toward the entrance. The door had barely closed behind them when he released her and bent forward, bracing his hands on his knees as a great roar of laughter burst from him. Madelyn collapsed over his back, seeing again the helpless, stunned look on the cowboy's face and the gleeful look on Floris's, and went off into helpless gales.

After her bad temper the laughter felt great. It was even more wonderful to hear Reese laughing, and a pang struck her as she realized that this was the first time she had heard him laugh. He rarely even smiled, but now he was hugging his ribs and wiping tears from his eyes, and still the deep sounds were booming up from his chest. She had an overwhelming urge to cry, but conquered it.

A lot of the tension between them dissolved as they bought groceries. Reese had been right; the general store did carry mostly basics, but Madelyn had carefully studied the cookbooks and knew what she could do with what was available. Thank God Reese wasn't a fussy eater.

A cheerful woman with a truly awesome bosom checked them out while carrying on a casual conversation with Reese. She eyed Madelyn questioningly, then looked down at the ring on her left hand. Reese saw the look and braced himself for the curiosity he knew would come. "Glenna, this is my wife, Madelyn."

Glenna looked startled, and her glance flew down to his own left hand. The gold ring on his tanned finger clearly astounded her. Reese carried on with the introduction, hoping to bridge her reaction. "Maddie, this is Glenna Kinnaird. We went to school together."

Recovering herself, Glenna beamed and held out her hand. "I can't believe it! Congratulations! You got married, after all this time. Why, just wait until I tell Boomer. We didn't really go to school together," she said chattily to Madelyn. "I'm ten years older than he is, so I graduated when he was in third grade, but I've known him all his life. How on earth did you catch him? I'd have sworn he'd never marry again— Uh, that is…" Her voice trailed off uneasily as she glanced at Reese.

Madelyn smiled. "It's okay. I know about April. As for how I caught him…well, I didn't. He caught me."

Glenna's face regained its cheerful expression. "Took one look and forgot about being a bachelor, huh?"

"Something like that," Reese said. He'd taken one look and gotten hard, but the end result had been the same: the leggy blonde with the lazy, seductive stroll was now his wife.

As they left the store with Glenna waving at them, he realized something that had him frowning thoughtfully as they loaded the groceries into the station wagon: Glenna had disliked April on sight, but had been perfectly comfortable and friendly with Madelyn. Even though, in an indescribable way, Madelyn dressed more fashionably than April, she had an easy, friendly manner to which Glenna had responded. Madelyn didn't dress as expensively as April, but what she wore had a certain style to it, as if she had practiced for hours to get her collar to stand up just so, or her sleeves to roll up that precise amount. She would always draw eyes, but she didn't inspire the sort of hostility from her own sex that April had.

Style. He looked at his wife and thought of how she'd looked the day before, with one kneepad slipping down her shin and her hair hanging in her face. He hadn't dared laugh then, but in retrospect he couldn't help himself and began to chuckle. Even when chasing chickens, Madelyn did it with style.

Madelyn had been outside all morning, scraping the peeling paint off the house. Having brought the interior up to snuff, she was working on the exterior, and it was such a beautiful morning that she'd been enjoying herself despite the hard work. It was getting close to noon, though, and the temperature was rising uncomfortably. Sweat was making her clothes stick to her. Deciding that she'd done enough for the day, she climbed down from the ladder and went inside to take a shower.

When she came back downstairs, the first thing she saw was the bag containing Reese's lunch sitting on the cabinet. He was out repairing fencing again and wouldn't be back until dinnertime, but he'd forgotten his lunch and thermos of tea.

She checked the clock. He had to be starving by now. Quickly she emptied the thermos and filled it with fresh ice cubes and tea, then got the keys to the station wagon and hurried outside with his lunch. By chance she knew where he was working, because in the past two weeks he'd shown her around the ranch a little, and he'd mentioned this morning where he'd be. It was actually a safety precaution for someone to know where he was, and she frowned as she thought of the years he'd worked alone, with no one at the house to know where he'd gone or how long he'd been out. If he'd gotten hurt, he could have lain there and died without anyone ever knowing he'd been hurt until it was too late.

Her marriage wasn't even three weeks old yet, and already she could barely remember her previous life. She'd never before been as busy as she was now, though she had to admit she would gladly forego the housework to ride around the ranch with Reese, but he still refused to hear of it. She was certain that if anyone looked up the word "stubborn" in the dictionary, it would have Reese Duncan's picture beside it.

He'd decided where she would fit in his life, and he wouldn't let her get outside that boundary.

She could almost feel the hunger in him at night when he made love to her, but he never let himself go, never released the passion she sensed, and as a result she couldn't let herself go, either. Sex was no longer uncomfortable, and she desperately wanted more from their lovemaking, but the intensity she needed wasn't there. He held back, diminishing the pleasure they both could have had and thereby preserving that damned inner wall of his. She didn't know how much longer she would be able to bear it, how much longer it would be before she began making excuses and turn away from him in the night. The situation was dire, she knew, when she was actually looking forward to having her period!

She drove slowly, preoccupied with her thoughts and with watching for any sign of his truck out on the range somewhere. Like all ranchers, Reese paid no attention to roads; he simply drove across the land. The truck was a tool to him, not a prized and pampered status symbol. If it had been a Rolls he would have treated it the same, because it had no value beyond that of its worth as a working vehicle. So she knew the area where he was working, but that area covered a lot of ground and he could be anywhere in it. She didn't see him anywhere, but fresh tire tracks scored the ground, and she simply followed them, carefully steering around the rougher ground that Reese had driven over without concern, because the station wagon was much lower than the truck and couldn't negotiate such terrain.

It took her almost forty-five minutes to find him. He'd parked the truck under a tree, partially shielding it from view. It was the chance glint off a strand of wire as he pulled it tight that caught her eye, and she eased the car across the range to him.

He glanced up briefly as she approached but didn't pause in his work. Her throat tightened. He'd removed his shirt and hung it over the side of the truck bed, and his muscled torso glistened with sweat. She'd known he was strong, realized from the first that his body made her mouth go dry with almost painful appreciation, but this was the first time she had seen those powerful muscles bunching and flexing like that. He moved with a fluid grace that made his strength that much more noticeable. His biceps and triceps bulged as he hammered a staple into the post, securing the new strand of wire.

When he was finished he tossed the hammer onto the sack of staples and pulled his hat off, wiping the sweat from his face with his forearm. "What are you doing out here?" He didn't sound at all pleased to see her.

Madelyn got out of the car, carrying the thermos and sandwiches with her. "You forgot your lunch."

He walked toward her and took the thermos, twisting the top off and tilting it up to drink directly from the spout. His strong throat worked as he swallowed the cold liquid. He'd been working all morning without anything to drink, she realized. A drop of tea escaped his lips and ran down his throat. She watched it in painful fascination as it slid down his hot skin, and she envied it the path it was taking. So often she had wanted to trail kisses down his body but had held back because he didn't want that sort of intimacy. All he wanted was the release of sex, not the love expressed in slow, sensual feasting.

He set the thermos down on the lowered tailgate and reached for his shirt, using it to wipe the sweat from his face, shoulders, arms and chest. Tossing the garment back across the side, he eased one hip onto the tailgate and took the sandwiches from her. "The station wagon isn't meant for driving across the range," he said as he unwrapped a sandwich.

Madelyn's lips tightened. "I didn't want you to go all day without anything to eat or drink, and I was careful."

"How did you find me?"

"I followed your tire tracks."

He grunted and applied himself to the sandwich. It and another disappeared without another word being said between them. Madelyn lifted her hair off her neck, letting a slight breeze cool her heated skin. She usually braided her hair away from her face during the day, but she'd taken it down when she showered and hadn't put it back up again before she'd started searching for Reese.

Reese watched her graceful gesture, and his heartbeat speeded up. She was wearing a gathered white cotton skirt with one of her favorite white camisole tops, and a pair of sandals that were little more than thin soles with a few delicate straps. She looked cool and fragrant, while he was hot and sweaty, a result of the difference in the way they'd spent the day. Now that the house was clean and polished it probably didn't take much to keep it that way.

The breeze caught a strand of hair and blew it across her face. She shook it back, tilting her head to make all of her hair swing down her back.

Every movement she made was naturally seductive. He felt the response in his groin and in his veins, as his blood heated and began racing. It was becoming more and more difficult to keep his hands off her during the day, to keep from turning to her time and again during the night. He grew angry at himself for wanting her so much, and at her for doing everything she could to make it worse.

"Why did you really come out here?" he asked harshly. "I would've finished with this and gotten back to the house in another hour or so. I've gone without eating or drinking all day before, and I'll do it again. So why did you really come parading out here?"

Madelyn's eyes narrowed as she slowly turned her head to look at him. She didn't say anything, and the combined anger and sexual frustration built up even more pressure in him.

"Do you want me to stop work and play with you? Can't you go a whole day without a man's attention? Maybe you thought we'd have a sexy little picnic out here and you'd get your skirt tossed."

She turned to fully face him, her eyes locked with his. Her words were slow and precise. "Why would I care? From what I can tell, sex isn't worth a walk across the yard, let alone chasing it down on the range. I've got better things to do with my time."

He took the verbal jab square on the ego, and suddenly it was too much. It was all too much, the wanting and not having, the needing and not taking. A red mist swam before his eyes, and his whole body seemed to expand as he blindly reached for her, catching her by the arm and swinging her up against him.

Madelyn was unprepared for the blurring speed with which he moved. She didn't even have time to take a step back. Suddenly he had her arm in a painful grip and with one motion brought her colliding with his hard body, almost knocking the breath from her. His mouth came down, hot and ravaging, not waiting for her compliance but taking it. His teeth raked across her bottom lip, and when she made a shaky sound of...response? protest? he used the opportunity to enter her mouth with his tongue.

Her heart lunged wildly in her chest as she realized he was out of control. His arms had tightened around her, lifting her off her feet, and his mouth took hers with bruising force. Elation swirled in her, and she wound her arms tightly around his neck as she kissed him back.

He hefted her onto the tailgate of the truck and reached for his shirt, tossing it down on the truck bed. With a motion so smooth it seemed like one movement he slid her backward and leaped to a crouching position on the tailgate; then he was pushing her down onto the shirt and lowering himself on top of her.

Dimly she realized that once you had unleashed a tiger, it wasn't so easy to get him back under control again. Of course, she wasn't sure she wanted to. The sunlight sifted down through the leaves, dappling his gleaming skin, and his eyes were fiercely primitive as he kneed her thighs apart. He looked wild and magnificent, and she made a soft whimpering sound of need as she reached for him.

He tore her clothes, and she didn't care. The seam of her chemise gave way beneath his twisting fingers, and the taut rise of her breasts thrust nakedly up at him. He sucked strongly at her while he shoved her skirt to her waist and hooked his fingers in the waistband of her underpants. She lifted her hips to aid him, but heard the rip of lace, and then he threw the shreds to one side. He transferred his lips to her other breast and sucked the nipple into his mouth while he worked at the fastening of his jeans. He grunted as the zipper parted, releasing his throbbing length, and he shoved both underwear and jeans downward with one movement.

His entry was hard and fast. Her body shuddered under the impact of it, and her hips lifted. He groaned aloud as the exquisite feminine sheath enveloped him, immediately changing his unbearable ache into unbearable pleasure.

Madelyn sank her nails into his back as she arched up, driven by an explosion of heat. Coiling tension tightened her body until she thought she would go mad, and she struggled with both him and the tension, crying out a little as her heaving body strained to throw him off even as her legs tightened around him to pull him deeper. If he was wild, so was she. He pounded into her, and she took him. Her hips hammered back at him and he rode her, wrapping his arms under her buttocks to pull her up tighter, to shove himself in deeper.

A great rolling surge exploded her senses without warning, and she gave a primal scream that sliced across the clear air. He kept thrusting heavily into her, and it happened again, the second time following the first so closely that she hadn't had time to regain her breath, and the second time was more powerful, tossing her even higher. She bit his shoulder, sobbing from the force of it, and suddenly she could feel him grow even harder and bigger inside her, and his entire body began shuddering and heaving. He threw back his head with a guttural cry that ripped up from his chest as his hips jerked in the spasms of completion.

The quiet afterward had a drifting, dreamy quality to it. She could feel the sunlight filtering down on her skin, the heat of the metal truck bed beneath her, his shirt pillowing her head. A bird sang, and a breeze rustled the leaves and grass. She could hear the faint buzzing of a bee somewhere, and the slowing sound of his breathing.

They lay beside each other, his heavy arm across her stomach. She might have dozed. The breeze dried the sweat on her body with a gentle, cooling touch. After a long, long time that might have been only minutes, she turned into his arms and pressed her mouth to his.

He got his boots and jeans off this time. As rawly frenzied as the first time had been, this one wasn't much less. The force of his restrained hunger had built up until, like a flooding river overwhelming a dam, it had broken through and could no longer be controlled. He undid her skirt and stripped it down her legs; then she parted her thighs and reached for him again, and he couldn't wait a minute longer. The sight of those sleek legs opening for him was an image that had haunted his dreams. He'd intended to be easier with her this time, but as soon as he penetrated she made a wild sound in her throat and her hips rolled, and he went mad again.

This time when it was over he didn't withdraw, but lay on her in continued possession. "Reese," she whispered, her fingers sliding into his damp hair. He slid his thumbs under her chin and tilted her face up, slanting his head so he could drink from her in the long, deep kisses he'd been craving. He began to grow hard again, but he was still inside her and there was no urgency, only steadily increasing pleasure.

They were both drugged with it. He fondled her breasts, caressing them with both hands and mouth. Her slim hands moved over him like silk, sleeking over his broad shoulders and down the taut muscles of his back, finally cupping and kneading his buttocks. Lifting himself on his arms, he began a slow, steady thrusting. She surged upward, too, kissing his throat and chest and licking at his little nipples, half-hidden in the curls of hair on his chest. When her time was close, she writhed on the twisted bed of clothing, and he watched enthralled as her torso flushed and her nipples tightened. He caught her hips and lifted them, sliding her up and down on his impaling flesh, and the sight of her convulsive satisfaction brought him to the peak before she had finished.

The hot midday hours slipped away as they sated themselves on each other's bodies. Nothing else existed but sensual exploration and hot satisfaction. He kissed her from head to toe, tasting the sweetness of her flesh, delighting in the way she responded to his slightest touch. When her back became tender from rubbing on the hard bed he pulled her on top of him, watching her pleasure at the freedom it gave her to take him at her own pace.

He thought he had to be completely empty, yet he couldn't stop. He didn't know if he'd ever be able to stop. The peaks were no longer shattering, but were slow, strong swells that seemed to last forever.

Madelyn clung to him, not thinking, never wanting to think. This was the magic she had wanted, the burning sensuality she had sensed in him. No part of her body was untouched, unloved. Exhaustion crept in and entwined with pleasure, and at some point they went to sleep.

The sun was low when they woke, and the air was getting cooler. Reese pulled her into the heat of his body and smoothed her hair back from her face. "Are you all right?" he murmured, concerned when he remembered the violent intensity of their lovemaking.

She nuzzled her face against his throat, lifting one slender arm to curl it around his neck. "Umm," she said and closed her eyes again. She didn't feel like moving.

He sleeked his hand over her hip and up her side, then cupped her breast. "Wake up, honey."

"I am awake." The words were slow and muffled against his throat.

"It's almost sunset. We need to go."

"We can sleep here." She moved as if trying to sink into his skin, and her own hand strayed downward. He closed his eyes as her fingers closed gently around him. Her lips opened against his throat, then slid upward to his jaw. "Make love to me again, Reese. Please."

"Don't worry about that," he said beneath his breath. There was no way he could restrain himself now that he'd tasted her passion, no way she would let him, now that she knew. With a mixture of anger and despair he knew he'd never be able to keep his hands off her now. But the temperature was getting cooler by the second as the sun began dipping below the horizon; even though he was tempted to lie there with her, he didn't want her to get chilled.

He sat up and drew her with him. "Home," he said, his voice roughening. "My knees have had about all they can take. I want to be in bed the next time."

Her eyes were slumberous, her lips swollen from his kisses. "As long as it's soon," she whispered, and thought she would cry, she loved him so much.

7

Her spirit was willing but her body went to sleep. She slept in his arms that night, her head on his shoulder and one leg thrown over his hip. Reese let her sleep, feeling the contentment of his own body as well as a certain wryness. If Madelyn had been seductive before, she was doubly so now. It was as if she had been holding back, too. That night, she hadn't walked past him without reaching out to touch him somewhere: a lingering hand sliding along his ribs, a gentle touch on his hand or arm, or a light ruffling of his hair, a tickle of his ear, a quick kiss on his chin, an appreciative pat on his butt, even a bold caress of his crotch. After denying himself for so long, he couldn't keep his hands off her, either. By the time he'd showered, eaten dinner and rested for an hour, the accumulated effect of all those caresses, both given and received, had had him hard and aching again. She had gone sweetly into his arms in bed, he'd made love to her, this time with lingering gentleness, and then she had gone to sleep before he'd withdrawn from her.

He'd stayed inside her for a long time, dozing himself and luxuriating in the intimacy. When he tried to move she muttered a protest and turned with him, burrowing against him and retaining the connection. So he hooked his arm around her bottom and kept her locked to him all night, and he slept better than he had since the day he'd met her.

He was on his back and she was sprawled on top of him when the alarm went off the next morning. He stretched to shut it off while she wiggled sleepily on his chest like a cat. He rubbed his hand down her back. "Time to get up."

His early-morning voice was dark and rough. Madelyn settled her head in the hollow of his shoulder again. "Did you know," she said sleepily, "that more words in the English language start with S than with any other letter?"

"Ah, God, not now," he groaned. "Not before coffee."

"Chicken."

"I don't want to talk about any damn chickens, either." He struggled to wake up. "Canada is over two hundred thousand square miles larger than the United States."

"A pound of feathers weighs more than a pound of gold because of the different weighing systems used."

"Catgut comes from sheep guts, not cat guts."

She jerked upright, frowning at him, and he used the opportunity to turn on the lamp. "No gross stuff," she ordered, then settled back down on his chest. "A blue whale's heart beats just nine times a minute."

"Robert E. Lee's family home is now Arlington National Cemetery."

"*Mona Lisa* doesn't have any eyebrows, and the real name of the painting is *La Gioconda*."

"Quicksand is more buoyant that water. Contrary to Hollywood, you'd really have to work at it to go completely under in quicksand."

She yawned and was silent, listening to his heartbeat, a strong, steady drumming in her ear. As she listened it began beating faster, and she raised her head to look at him. His eyes were narrowed and intent. He locked his arms around her and rolled until she was beneath him, his legs between hers and spreading them wide. Madelyn clung to him and gave herself up to the now-familiar rise of ecstasy as he began making love to her.

"What are you doing today?" she asked over breakfast.

"Moving a portion of the herd to another section so they won't overgraze."

"I'm going with you."

He automatically started to refuse, and she gave him a hard look. "Don't say no," she warned. "I've already got steaks marinating in the refrigerator, and the baked potatoes are almost done, so they'll finish baking while the steaks are grilling. There's no reason for me to sit here every day when I can be with you."

"What I wonder," he muttered, "is if I'll get any work done at all. All right, I'll saddle a horse for you. But I'm warning you, Maddie, if you can't ride well enough to keep up, you won't go out with me again."

She showed up at the barn half an hour later wearing jeans, boots and one of his denim workshirts with the sleeves rolled up and the tails tied in a knot at her waist. Her hair was French-braided in one long braid down the center of her back, she wore a new pair of wrist-length gloves, and she looked as chic as if she were modeling clothes rather than heading out for a day of herding cattle. She carried a western straw hat and settled it on her head before she approached the horse Reese had saddled for her.

He watched as she gave the animal time to get acquainted with her, letting it snuffle at her arms, scratching it behind its ears. She wasn't afraid of horses, at least. April had never been around them, and as a result had been jumpy in their vicinity, which in turn made the horses skittish. Madelyn petted the horse and crooned to it, then untied the reins, put her boot in the stirrup and competently swung into the saddle. Reese eyed the stirrups and decided he had judged the length correctly, then mounted his own horse.

He watched her carefully as they cantered across a field. She had a good seat and nice steady hands, though she lacked the easy posture he possessed, but he'd been riding since he was a toddler. The smile she gave him was so full of pleasure he felt guilty at not taking her with him before.

He set an easy pace, not wanting to push her too hard. When they reached the herd he explained how he worked. The herd was already divided into three smaller groups grazing different sections; the entire herd was too big for him to move by himself. He spent a lot of time moving them to fresh grazing and making certain they didn't destroy the plant cycle by overgrazing. He pointed out the bunch they would be moving and gave her a coiled section of rope. "Just wave it alongside the horse's shoulder in a shooing motion, and let the horse do the work if a cow decides to go in a different direction. All you have to do is sit deep in the saddle and hang on."

Sitting deep in the saddle was no problem; the big western rig felt like a cradle after the small eastern saddle she was familiar with. She took the coil of rope and practiced a few waves with it, just to be certain it didn't startle the horse. He treated it as commonplace, which, of course, to him it was.

She enjoyed the work. She liked being outside, and there was a sort of peace to riding alongside the cattle and waving a coil of rope at them occasionally, listening to the deep-throated bawls and learning the joy of riding a well-trained cutting horse. She liked watching Reese most of all. He had been born to do this, and it was obvious in every movement and sound he made. He rode as if he were a part of the horse, anticipating every change of direction, encouraging the cattle with whistles and calls that seemed to reassure them at the same time.

She felt almost dazed with pleasure, her senses overloaded. She had felt that way since the afternoon before, when his self-control had broken and he had taken her like a man possessed. Her body was sated, her emotions freed to reach out to him and shower him with the love that had been dammed up inside her. She had no illusions that the battle was won, but the first skirmish was hers; until yesterday, he would never have allowed her to pet him as she had been doing, nor would he have lingered in bed that morning to make love again. His face was still set in those stern, unsmiling lines, but he was subtly more relaxed. Judging from the past twenty-four hours, he must have had a difficult time controlling his sex drive. The thought made her smile.

They stopped for lunch and to let the cattle and horses drink from a small natural pond. When the horses had been seen to, Reese tethered them nearby and sat down next to her on the small rise she'd chosen for the site of their meal. He took off his hat and put it on the grass beside him. "How do you like it so far?"

"A lot." Her lips curved softly as she handed him a sandwich. "It's so peaceful out here, no cars, no telephones, no smog. You may have to help me out of bed in the morning, but it'll be worth it."

"I'll rub you down with liniment tonight." His eyes glinted at her. "Afterward."

That statement earned him a kiss. Then she straightened and unwrapped her own sandwich. "How am I doing? Have I done anything totally amateurish?"

"You're doing fine. The only problem is that I keep worrying you're going to get tossed and stepped on. You're the first female cowhand I've ever had."

He was very western in his attitude toward women, but she didn't mind him coddling her as long as he didn't also try to stop her from doing what she wanted. Since he was bound to do that, their lives together should never become too complacent.

He propped himself on one elbow and stretched his long legs out as he ate his second sandwich. She began to feel warm as she watched him; though he was simply dressed in brown jeans, a white shirt and those disreputably scuffed boots, he outshone male models she'd seen in tuxedos. His first wife had to be president of a Stupid Club somewhere, but the wretched woman shouldn't be allowed to get away with what she'd done to him. Madelyn had never before thought of herself as vindictive, but she felt that way about anyone who had ever harmed Reese. If she ever met April, she would snatch her bald-headed.

He found the cookies she'd packed and washed them down with the last of the tea. Feeding this man could be a full-time job, she thought fondly. If his children inherited his appetite, she'd never get out of the kitchen.

Thinking of having his children made her feel even warmer, but reminded her of something she'd meant to discuss with him. She turned to face him, sitting with her legs folded in front of her.

"There's something we have to talk about."

"What's that?" he asked, stretching out on his back and settling his hat over his eyes.

"Children."

One eye opened and peered at her; then he removed the hat and gave her his full attention. "Ye gods, are you already pregnant?"

"No, and even if I were, I wouldn't know yet, because it isn't time for my period. We didn't talk about it before we got married, so I didn't know if you wanted to wait before we had children or if you wanted to have them right away. When you called, it was almost time for my period, so when I went to the doctor for the physical I got a prescription for birth control pills."

He sat up, his face darkening. "You're on the Pill?"

"Yes. I've only taken it for this month. If you want to start trying to have children right away, I can stop."

"You should have discussed it with me before, or was that another one of those subjects, like your virginity, that you didn't think were any of my business?''

She gave him one of those sidelong glances. "Something like that. I didn't know you, and I didn't feel very comfortable with you."

He watched her for a minute, then reached out to take her hand, rubbing his rough thumb over her soft palm. "How do you feel about getting pregnant right away?"

"I wouldn't mind. I want your children. If you want to wait, that's okay with me, too, but I don't want to wait more than a year. I'm twenty-eight. I don't want to be in my mid-thirties when we get started."

He thought about it while he studied the contrast of her delicate hand in his big, rough one. Now that he'd given in to the powerful physical attraction between them, he didn't want to give it up too soon. He wanted to fully enjoy her for a while before pregnancy put necessary limits on the wildness of their lovemaking. He carried her hand to his mouth and licked her palm. "Take the Pill for a few months," he said. "We'll talk about it again in the fall."

She shivered, a dazed expression coming into her eyes at the stroke of his tongue on her palm. As he pulled her down on the grass she asked, "Do you think you'll get your boots off this time?"

And he replied, "I doubt it."

He didn't, but she didn't care.

She went with him often after that. She helped him move cattle, inoculate them, and staple tags in their ears. After he'd cut and baled the hay, she drove the truck pulling the hay trailer around while he swung the heavy bales onto it. It was work that really required a third person, to stack the bales, but it was easier than when Reese had had to do it by himself. When she didn't go out with him, she continued with the project of scraping the house.

He finally noticed the difference in the house and investigated. The dusting of white paint chips on the ground told him all he needed to know.

He leaned against the kitchen cabinet and crossed his arms. "Are you scraping the house?"

"Yep."

"Don't pull the Gary Cooper routine on me. I want it stopped right now."

"The routine or the scraping?"

"Both."

"The house can't be painted until the old paint is scraped off," she said reasonably.

"I can't afford the paint, so it doesn't make any difference. And I don't want you climbing around on a fourteen-foot ladder. What if you fell while I'm out on the range?"

"What if you got hurt out on the range by yourself?" she retorted. "I'm careful, and I haven't had any trouble so far. It shouldn't take too much longer."

"No," he said, enunciating carefully. "I can't afford the paint, and even if I could I wouldn't let you do the scraping."

"*You* don't have time for it, so who else is going to do it?"

"For the third time," he yelled, "*I can't afford the paint!* What does it take to make you understand that?"

"That's something else we've never talked about. What makes you think *we* can't afford the paint? I supported myself before I married you, you know." She put her hands on her hips and faced off with him. "I have both a checking and a savings account, which I transferred to a bank in Billings. I also have a trust fund that I inherited from Grandma Lily. It isn't a fortune by any means, but we can certainly afford a few gallons of paint!"

Reese's face was like granite. "No. Remember our prenuptial agreement? What's yours is yours and what's mine is mine. If you spent your money on the ranch it would go a long way toward negating that agreement, giving you a claim to it on the basis of up-keep."

She poked him in the chest, her jaw jutting forward. "For one thing, G. Reese Duncan, *I'm* not planning on getting a divorce, so I don't give a flip what's in your precious agreement. For another, how much would it cost to paint the house? A hundred dollars? Two hundred?"

"Closer to two hundred, and no, by God, you're not buying the paint!"

"I'm not only going to buy it, I'm going to paint it! If you're so set on protecting the ranch from my scheming, then we'll draw up a contract where you agree to repay me for the paint—and my time, too, if you insist—and that will take care of any claim I could make against you. But I live here, too, you know, and I want the outside to look as nice as the inside. Next spring I'm planting flowers in the flower beds, so if you object to that we might as well fight it out now. The only choice you have right now is the color you want the house painted, and your choices are white and white.'' She was yelling by the time she finished, her face flushed.

He was more furious than she'd ever seen him before. "Do whatever the hell you want,'' he snapped and slammed out of the kitchen.

She did. The next time they went into town she bought the paint and brushes and paid for them with one of her own checks, glaring at him and daring him to start again. He carried the paint out to the truck with ill grace. The high point of that day was when they stopped at the café for coffee and listened to Floris berating her customers.

She had the house painted by the middle of August, and had developed a healthy respect for people who painted houses for a living. It was some of the hardest work she'd ever done, leaving her shoulders and arms aching by the end of the day. The most aggravating part was painting the hundreds of thin porch railings; the most nerve-racking was doing the second floor, because she had to anchor herself to something. But when it was finished and the house gleamed like a jewel, and the shutters wore a new coat of black all-weather enamel, she was prouder of her efforts than she had ever been before of anything she'd done.

Even Reese grudgingly admitted that the house looked nice and she'd done a good job, but he still resented the fact that she'd done it. Maybe it was only male pride, but he didn't want his wife paying for something when he couldn't afford it himself.

His wife. By the time they had been married two months, she had insinuated herself so completely into his life that there wasn't a portion of it she hadn't touched. She had even rearranged his underwear drawer. Sometimes he wondered how she managed to accomplish as much as she did when her pace seldom exceeded a stroll, but it was a fact that she got things done. In her own way she worked as hard as he did.

One hot morning at the end of August she discovered that she didn't have enough flour to do the day's cooking. Reese had already left for the day and wouldn't be coming back for lunch, so she ran upstairs and got ready. It was almost time they replenished their supplies anyway, so she carried the grocery list with her. It would save an extra trip if she did all the shopping while she was in town.

She loved listening to Floris, so she stopped by the café and had coffee and pie. After Floris had sent her only other customer stomping out in anger, she came over to Madelyn's booth and sat down.

"Where's that man of yours today?"

"Out on the range. I ran out of flour and came in to stock up."

Floris nodded approvingly, though her sour face never lightened. "That first wife of his never bought no groceries. Don't guess she knew nothing about cooking, though of course Reese had a cook hired back then. It's a shame what happened to that ranch. It used to be a fine operation."

"It will be again," Madelyn said with confidence. "Reese is working hard to build it back up."

"One thing about him, he's never been afraid of work. Not like some men around here." Floris glared at the door as if she could still see the cowboy who had just left.

After talking with Floris, Glenna's cheerfulness was almost culture shock. They chatted for a while; then Madelyn loaded the groceries into the station wagon and drove back to the ranch. It wasn't quite noon, so she would have plenty of time to cook the cake she'd planned.

To her surprise, Reese's truck was in the yard when she drove up. He was coming around from the back of the house carrying a bucket of water, but when he saw her, he changed direction and stalked over, his face dark with temper and his eyes shooting green sparks. "Where in hell have you been?" he roared.

She didn't like his manner, but she answered his question in a reasonable tone. "I didn't have enough flour to do the cooking today, so I drove to Crook and bought groceries."

"Damn it, don't you ever go off without telling me where you're going!"

She retained her reasonableness, but it was becoming a strain. "How could I tell you when you weren't here?"

"You could have left a note."

"Why would I leave a note when you weren't supposed to be back for lunch, and I'd be back long before you? Why *are* you back?"

"One of the hoses sprang a leak. I came back to put a new hose on." For whatever reason, he wasn't in a mood to let it go. "If I hadn't, I wouldn't have found out you've started running around the country on your own, would I? How long has this been going on?"

"Buying food? Several centuries, I'd say."

Very carefully he put the bucket down. As he straightened, Madelyn saw his eyes; he wasn't just angry or aggravated, he was in a rage. He hadn't been this angry before, even over painting the house. With his teeth clenched he said, "You dressed like that to buy groceries?"

She looked down at her clothes. She wore a slim pink skirt that ended just above her knees and a white silk blouse with the sleeves rolled up. Her legs were bare, and she had on sandals. "Yes, I dressed like this to buy groceries! It's hot, in case you haven't noticed. I didn't want to wear jeans, I wanted to wear a skirt, because it's cooler."

"Did you get a kick out of men looking at your legs?"

"As far as I noticed, no one looked at my legs. I told you once that I won't pay for April's sins, and I meant it. Now, if you don't mind, I need to get the groceries into the house."

He caught her arm as she turned away and whirled her back around to face him. "Don't walk away when I'm talking to you."

"Well excuse me, Your Majesty!"

He grabbed her other arm and held her in front of him. "If you want to go to town, I'll take you," he said in an iron-hard voice. "Otherwise, you keep your little butt here on the ranch, and don't you ever, *ever*, leave the house without letting me know where you are."

She went up on tiptoe, so angry she was shaking. "Let me tell you a few things, and you'd better listen. I'm your wife, not your prisoner of war. I won't ask your permission to buy groceries, and I won't be kept locked up here like some criminal. If you take the keys to the car or do something to it so it won't run, then

I'll walk wherever I want to go, and you can bet the farm on that. I'm not April, do you understand? *I'm not April.*"

He released her arms, and they stood frozen, neither of them giving an inch. Very deliberately Madelyn bent down and lifted the bucket of water, then upended it over him. The water splashed on his head and shoulders and ran down his torso, to finally end up pooling around his boots.

"If that isn't enough to cool you off, I can get another one," she offered in an icily polite tone.

His movements were just as deliberate as hers as he removed his hat and slapped it against his leg to rid it of excess water, then dropped it to the ground. She saw his teeth clench; then he moved like a snake striking, his hands darting out to grasp her around the waist. With one swift movement he lifted her and plonked her down on the front fender of the car.

His hands were flexing on her waist; his forearms were trembling with the force it took to restrain his temper. His dark hair was plastered to his skull; water still dripped down his face, and his eyes were pure green fire.

His dilemma nearly tore him apart. He was trembling with rage, but there wasn't a damn thing he could do about it. His wife didn't back down from anyone, not even him, and he'd cut off his own hands before he would do anything to hurt her. All he could do was stand there and try to get his temper back under control.

They faced each other in silence for nearly a minute, with him still holding her on the fender of the car. She tilted her chin, her eyes daring him to start the fight again. He looked down at her legs, and a shudder ran through him. When he looked back up at her, it wasn't rage in his eyes.

Green eyes locked with gray. He hooked his fingers in the hem of her skirt and jerked it upward, at the same time spreading her legs and moving forward between them. She sank her hands into his wet hair and held his head while her mouth attacked his with a fierce kiss that held mingled anger and desire. He said, "Maddie," in a rough tone as he tore her underpants out of the way, then jerked at his belt and the fastening of his jeans.

It was just as it had been in the back of the truck. The rush of passion was hard and fast and overwhelming. With one hand he guided himself, while the other propelled her hips forward onto him. She moaned and wrapped her legs around him, then held his head so that their eyes met again. "I love you," she said fiercely. "I love you, damn it."

The words hit him like a thunderbolt, but her eyes were clear and direct, and he was losing himself in her depths. What had begun wild suddenly turned slow and hot and tender. He put his hand in her hair and tugged her head back to expose the graceful arch of her throat to his searching mouth. He began moving within her, probing deep and slow, and he said, "Maddie," again, this time in a voice that shook.

She was like fire, and she was all his. She burned for him and with him, her intense sensuality matching his. They clung together, savoring the hot rise of passion and the erotic strokes that fed it and would eventually extinguish it, but not now. Not right now.

He unbuttoned her blouse while she performed the same service for his shirt. When he had unclipped her bra he slowly brought their bare torsos together, turning her slightly from side to side so that her breasts rubbed his chest and his curly hair rasped against her nipples, making her arch in his arms.

"God, I can't get enough of you," he muttered.

"I don't want you to." Passion had glazed her eyes, making them heavy and slumberous. He took her mouth again, and he was still kissing her when she cried out and convulsed in a crest of pleasure. He held himself deep within her, feeling the hot, gentle tightening of her inner caresses around him. He would never find this kind of overwhelming passion with any other woman, he thought dimly. Only with Maddie.

Release left her weak, pliable. She lay back across the hood of the car, breathing hard, her eyes closed. Reese gripped her hips and began thrusting hard and fast, wanting that sweet weakness for himself. Her eyes slowly opened as he drove into her, and she closed her hands around his wrists. "I love you," she said again.

Until he heard the words once more he hadn't realized how badly he'd needed them, wanted them. She was his, and had been from the moment she'd walked through the airport toward him. He groaned, and his hips jerked; then the pleasure hit him, and he couldn't think for a long time. All he could do was feel, and sink forward onto her soft body and into her arms.

In bed that night, he gently traced his fingertips over the curve of her shoulder. "I'm sorry," he murmured. "I was out of line today, way out."

She kissed him drowsily on the jaw. "I think I understand more than before. Did April . . . ?"

"Have other men? Yeah."

"The fool," she muttered, sliding her hand down to intimately caress him.

He tilted her head up. "I wasn't a saint, Maddie. I can be hard to live with."

She widened her eyes mockingly and made a disbelieving sound. He chuckled and then sighed, spreading his legs. What her hand was doing to him felt so good it was almost criminal. She was all woman, and this was going to end up only one way, but he wanted to put it off for a few minutes.

"You're right, I've been trying to keep you a prisoner on the ranch. It won't happen again."

"I'm not going to run off," she assured him in a whisper. "I've got what I want right here. And you were right about one thing."

"What?"

"Making love is one of the best ways to make up."

8

Reese sold the beef herd for more than he had antic- ipated, or even hoped. With cholesterol-consciousness at such a high level he had been working to breed and raise cattle with leaner meat that still remained tender, and all his research was paying off. He made his mortgage payments with grim satisfaction, because he had enough left over to expand the herd come spring and bring in some new blood strains he'd been want- ing to try. He'd be able to repair equipment when it needed it, instead of scraping and saving and doing without. He'd even be able to take Madelyn out to eat once in a while. It galled him that the limit of their outside entertainment was an occasional cup of cof- fee or slice of pie at Floris's café. He wanted to be able to take Madelyn places and spoil her, buy her new clothes and jewelry, all the things he had once taken for granted in his life. The ranch was a long way from being as rich as it had once been, but he was clawing his way back. He'd made a profit, by God! He was in the black.

Madelyn had gone into Billings with him when he conferred with his banker. He'd expected her to want to go shopping; though he realized more every day how different Maddie was from April, he also wryly accepted that his wife was a clotheshorse. The fact that she loved clothes was evident in the way she dressed even while working at the ranch. It might be just jeans and a shirt, but the jeans would fit her in a way guaranteed to send his blood pressure up, and the shirt would look as stylish as if it had come straight from Paris. What really got to him was the way she would put on one of his white dress shirts, not button *any* of the buttons, and knot the tails at her waist. She wouldn't have a bra on under it, either. It was a style and a provocation that he couldn't resist, and she knew it. First his hand would be inside the shirt; then the shirt would be off; then they would be making love wherever they happened to be.

She did shop, but again she surprised him. She bought underwear and jeans for him; then she was ready to go home. "I don't know how I ever stood a city as large as New York," she said absently, looking around at the traffic. "This is too noisy." He was astonished; Billings had less than seventy thousand inhabitants, and barroom brawls were far more the norm than any gang- or drug-related violence. No, Maddie wasn't like April, who had considered Billings nothing more than a backwater crossroads. To April, only cities like New York, London, Paris, Los Angeles and Hong Kong had been sophisticated enough for her enjoyment.

Madelyn was indeed glad to get back to the ranch. She was happiest there, she realized. It was quiet, with the peace that came only from being close to earth and nature. And it was her home now.

It was the middle of the afternoon when they got back, and Reese changed clothes to begin his chores. It was too early to start dinner, so Madelyn went out on the porch and sat in the swing. It was early autumn, and already the heat was leaving the day. Reese said it wasn't unusual to have snow in October, so the days when she would be able to sit out on the porch were limited. Still, she was looking forward to the winter, hard as it might be. The days would be short and the nights long, and she smiled as she thought of those long nights.

Reese came back downstairs from changing his clothes and found her there. The chores would wait a little while, he thought, and joined her on the swing. He put his arm around her and brought her closer, so that her head was nestled in the hollow of his shoulder.

"I was just thinking," she said, "It'll be winter soon."

"Sooner than you think."

"Christmas isn't that far away now. Could I invite Robert?"

"Of course. He's your family."

She smiled. "I know, but the warmth between you at our wedding wasn't exactly overwhelming."

"What did you expect, given the circumstances? Men are territorial. He didn't want to give you up, and I was determined to have you come hell or high water." He nudged her chin up with his thumb and gave her a slow kiss. "And I was a stranger who was going to be taking his sister to bed that night."

For a moment there was only the creaking of the swing. He kissed her again, then just held her. He hadn't known marriage could be like this, he thought with vague surprise. Both passion and contentment.

He said quietly, "Let's have a baby."

After a pause she said, "I'll stop taking the Pill." Then she reached for his hand and cradled it to her face.

The tenderness of the gesture was almost painful. He lifted her up and settled her astride his lap so he could see her expression. "Is that what you want?"

Her face looked as if it had been lit from within. "You know it is." She leaned forward and brushed his lips with hers, then suddenly laughed and threw her arms around his neck, fiercely hugging him. "Are there any twins in your family?"

"No!" he said explosively, then drew back and gave her a suspicious look. "Are there in yours?"

"Actually, yes. Grandma Lily was a twin."

Even the thought of twins was too much. He shook his head, denying the possibility. "Just one at a time, gal. No doubling up." He rubbed his hands up her thighs and under her skirt, then slid them inside her underpants to cup her bare buttocks. "You might be pregnant by Christmas."

"Umm, I'd like that."

His eyes glinted at her. "I'll do my best."

"But it'll probably take longer than that."

"Then I'll just have to try harder."

Her lips quirked. "I can't lose," she said in contentment.

The first snow did come in October, three inches of fine, dry powder. She learned that snow didn't stop a rancher's work, it only intensified it, though three inches was nothing to worry about. In the dead of winter Reese would have to carry hay to the cattle and break the ice in the stock ponds so they could drink.

He'd have to find lost calves before they froze to death and move the herd to more sheltered areas during the worst weather.

For the first time, winter began to worry her. "What if there are blizzard conditions?" she asked him one night.

"Then I hope for the best," he said flatly. "I'll lose some calves during any bad snowstorm, but if it doesn't last too long the biggest part of the herd will weather it. The danger is if blizzard conditions or extreme cold last for several days. Then the cattle start freezing to death, and during a blizzard I can't get feed out to them. I have hooks attached to the barn and the house. When it looks like a bad storm, I run a static line between them and hook myself to it so I can get back and forth to the barn."

She stared at him, appalled at the years he'd coped by himself and the danger he'd been in. It was testimony to his strength and intelligence that he was still alive, and characteristic of his stubbornness that he'd even tried.

The preparations for winter were ongoing and not to be taken lightly. He moved the herd to the closer pastures where they would winter. Cords of firewood were stacked close to the back door, and the pantry was well stocked with candles and batteries, while he cleaned and tested two big kerosene heaters in case they were needed. The truck and car were both filled with new antifreeze and given new batteries, and he began parking them in the garage to keep them out of the wind. During October the temperature steadily slipped lower, until the only time it was above freezing was at high noon.

"Does it stay below freezing for six months?" she asked, and he laughed.

"No. We'll have cold spells and warm spells. It may be sixty degrees or higher in January, but if we get blizzard conditions or a deep freeze the temperatures can go way below zero. We prepare for a blizzard and hope for the sixty degrees."

As if to bear him out, the weather then showed a warming trend and inched the temperatures upward into the fifties during the day. Madelyn felt more confident, because he'd been making preparations as if they were going into six months of darkness. That was how he'd made it by himself for seven years, by being cautious and prepared for anything. Still, by his own admission the winters could be hell. She would just have to make certain he didn't take any chances with his own safety.

Robert flew in the day before Christmas and spent three days with them. When he first saw Madelyn he gave her a hard, searching look, but whatever he saw must have reassured him, because he relaxed then and was an affable guest. She was amused at the way Reese and Robert related to each other, since they were so much alike, both very private and strong men. Their conversation consisted of sentence fragments, as if they were just throwing out random comments, but they both seemed comfortable with it. She was amazed at how much alike they were in manner, too. Robert was smoothly cosmopolitan, yet Reese's mannerisms were much like his, illustrating how prosperous the ranch had been before the divorce. They differed only in that she had never seen Robert lose his temper, while Reese's temper was like a volcano.

Robert was surprisingly interested in the working of the ranch and rode out with Reese every day he was there. They spent a lot of time talking about futures and stock options, the ratio of feed to pound of beef, interest rates, inflation and government subsidies. Robert looked thoughtful a lot, as if he were weighing everything Reese said.

The day before he left, Robert approached Madelyn. She was sprawled bonelessly across a big armchair, listening to the stereo with her eyes closed and one foot keeping time to the music. He said in amusement, "Never run if you can walk, never walk if you can stand, never stand if you can sit, and never sit if you can lie."

"Never talk if you can listen," Madelyn added without opening her eyes.

"Then you listen, and I'll talk."

"This sounds serious. Are you going to tell me you're in love with someone and are thinking of marriage?"

"Good God, no," he said, his amusement deepening.

"Is there a new woman on the horizon?"

"A bit closer than that."

"Why didn't you bring her? Is it anyone I know?"

"This is a family Christmas," he replied, telling her with that one short sentence that his new lover hadn't touched him any deeper than any of the others. "Her name is Natalie VanWein."

"Nope. I don't know her."

"You're supposed to listen while I talk, not ask questions about my love life." He drew up a hassock and sat down on it, smiling a little as he noticed that she hadn't even opened her eyes during their conversation.

"So talk."

"I've never met anyone with a clearer head for business than Reese—excepting myself, of course," he said mockingly.

"Oh, of course."

"Listen, don't talk. He sees what has to be done and he does it, without regard to obstacles. He has the kind of determination that won't give up, no matter what the odds. He'll make a go of this ranch. He'll fight like hell until he has it the way it used to be."

Madelyn opened one eye. "And the point of this is?"

"I'm a businessman. He strikes me as a better risk than a lot of ventures I've bet on. He doesn't have to wait to build this place up. He could accept an investor and start right now."

"The investor, of course, being yurself."

He nodded. "I look for a profit. He'd make one. I want to invest in it personally, without involving Cannon Companies."

"Have you already talked to him about it?"

"I wanted to talk to you first. You're his wife, you know him better than I do. Would he go for it, or would I be wasting my time?"

"Well, I won't give you an opinion either way. You're on your own. Like you said, he knows the business, so let him make up his own mind without having to consider anything I might have said either pro or con."

"It's your home, too."

"I'm still learning to help, but I don't know enough about the business of ranching to even begin to make an educated decision. And when it comes down to it, my home is based on my marriage, not where we live. We could live anywhere and I'd be content."

He looked down at her, and a strangely tender look entered his pale eyes. "You're really in love with him, aren't you?"

"I have been from the beginning. I never would have married him otherwise."

He examined her face closely, in much the same way he'd looked at her when he had first arrived, as if satisfying himself of the truth of her answer. Then he gave a brusque nod and got to his feet. "Then I'll put the proposition to Reese and see what he thinks."

Reese turned it down, as Madelyn had expected he would. The ranch was his; it might take longer and be a harder fight to do it on his own, but every tree and every speck of dirt on the ranch belonged to him, and he refused to risk even one square inch of it with an outside investor. Robert took the refusal in good humor, because business was business, and his emotions were never involved any more than they were with women.

Reese talked to her about it that night, lying in the darkness with her head pillowed on his shoulder. "Robert made me an offer today. If I took him as an investor, I could double the ranch's operation, hire enough hands to work it and probably get back most of the former acreage within five years."

"I know. He talked to me about it, too."

He stiffened. "What did you tell him?"

"To talk to you. It's your ranch, and you know more about running it than anyone else."

"Would you rather I took his offer?"

"Why should I care?"

"Money," he said succinctly.

"I'm not doing without anything." Her voice had a warm, amused tone to it.

"You could have a lot more."

"I could have a lot less, too. I'm happy, Reese. If you took the offer I'd still be happy, and I'll still be happy if you don't take it."

"He said you wouldn't take sides."

"That's right, I won't. It would be a no-win situation for me, and I don't waste my energy."

He lay awake long after she was sleeping quietly in his arms. It was a way to instant financial security, but it would require that he do something he'd sworn never to do: risk ownership of the ranch. He already had a mortgage, but he was managing to make the payments. If he took an investor he would be paying off the bank but taking on another debtor, at a price he might not be able to meet. The big lure of it was that, perversely, he wanted to give Madelyn all the luxuries he would have been able to provide before.

To take care of his wife as he wanted, he'd have to risk his ranch. He didn't miss the irony of it.

The day after Robert left, a big weather system swept in from Canada and it began snowing. At first it was just snow, but it didn't stop. The temperature began dropping like a rock, and the wind picked up. Reese watched the weather build into something nasty, and the weather reports said it would get worse. While he still could, he herded the cattle into the most sheltered area and put out as much hay as possible, but he wasn't certain he'd had enough time to get out as much as would be needed.

On the way back to the barn it started snowing so heavily that visibility dropped to about ten feet, and the wind began piling up drifts that masked the shape of the land. His own ranch became an alien landscape to him, without any familiar landmarks to guide him. All he could go on was his own sense of direction, and he had to fight to ignore the disorienting swirl of snow. His horse picked its way carefully, trying to avoid the snow-covered holes and indentations that could easily cause it to fall and perhaps break a leg. Icicles began to form on the horse's nose as the warm vapor of its breath froze. Reese put a gloved hand to his own face and found it coated with ice crystals.

A ride that normally took twenty minutes stretched into an hour. He began to wonder if he had missed the barn entirely when it materialized out of the blowing snow, and even then he would have missed it if the door hadn't been open revealing the gleam of yellow light. A brief frown creased his face; he knew he'd closed the door, and he certainly hadn't left a light on. But it had been too close a call for him to be anything but grateful; another half hour and he wouldn't have made it.

He ducked his head and rode straight into the barn. It wasn't until he caught movement out of the corner of his eye that he realized Madelyn had come out to the barn and was waiting for him, literally with a light in the window. She struggled against the wind to close the big doors, her slender body leaning into the teeth of the gale. The cow bawled restlessly, and the cats leaped for the loft. Reese slid out of the saddle and added his weight to Madelyn's, closing the doors and dropping the big two-by-eight bar into the brackets.

"What the hell are you doing out here?" he asked in a raspy voice as he grabbed her to him. "Damn it, Maddie, you can get lost going from the house to the barn in a blow like this!"

"I hooked up to the tension line," she said, clinging to him. Her voice was thin. "How did you get back? You can't see out there."

He felt the panic in her, because he'd begun feeling some of it himself. If he'd been five feet farther away, he wouldn't have seen the light. "Sheer blind luck," he said grimly.

She looked up at his ice-crusted face. "You have to get warm before frostbite starts."

"The horse first."

"I'll do it." She pointed toward the tack room, where he kept a small space heater. "I turned on the heater so it would be warm in there. Now, go on."

Actually, the barn felt warm to him after being outside; the animals gave off enough heat that the temperature inside the barn was above freezing, which was all that he required right now. Still, he went into the tack room and felt the heat envelop him almost unbearably. He didn't try to brush the ice from his face; he let it melt, so it wouldn't damage his skin. It had actually insulated his face from the wind, but too much longer would have resulted in frostbite. He'd had mild cases before, and it was painful enough that he'd rather not go through it again.

Madelyn unsaddled the horse and rubbed it down. The big animal sighed with pleasure in a way that was almost human. Then she threw a warm blanket over it and gave it feed and water, patting the muscled neck in appreciation. The animal had earned it.

She hurried to Reese and found him knocking chunks of snow off his heavy shearling coat. That shocking white layer of ice and snow was gone from his face; what was almost as shocking was that he already seemed to have recovered his strength, as if the ordeal had been nothing out of the ordinary. She had been in torment since the howling wind had started, pacing the house and trying not to weep uncontrollably, and finally fighting her way out to the barn so she would be there to help him if—no, *when*—he made it back. Her heart was still pounding. She didn't have to be told how easily he might not have made it back, even though she couldn't bear to let the thought form.

"It won't be easy getting back to the house," he said grimly. "The wind is probably gusting up to sixty miles an hour. We'll both hook on to the line, but I'm going to tie you to me as a safeguard."

He knotted a rope around his waist, then looped and knotted it around her, with no more than four feet of slack between them. "I want you within reach. I'm going to try to hold on to you, but I damn sure don't want you getting any farther away from me than this."

He put his coat back on and settled his hat firmly on his head. He eyed Madelyn sternly. "Don't you have a hat?"

She produced a thick woolen scarf from her pocket and draped it over her head, then wound the ends around her neck. They each got a length of nylon cord

with heavy metal clips on each end and attached one
end to their belts, leaving the other end free to clip to
the line. They left the barn by the small side door;
though the line was anchored right beside it, Reese had
to grab Madelyn by the waist to keep the wind from
tumbling her head over heels. Still holding her, he
grabbed her line and hooked it overhead, then se-
cured his own.

It was almost impossible to make headway. For
every yard they progressed, stumbling and fighting,
the wind would knock them back two feet. It tore her
out of his grasp and knocked her feet out from under
her, hanging her in the air from the line at her waist.
Reese lunged for her, yelling something that she
couldn't understand, and hauled her against him. It
was obvious she wasn't going to be able to stay on her
feet. He locked her against his side with a grip that
compressed her ribs, almost shutting off her breath.
She gasped for air, but couldn't manage more than a
painful wheeze. She couldn't have yelled to make him
understand, even if she'd had the breath, because the
howling wind drowned out everything else. She dan-
gled in his grip like a rag doll, her sight fading and her
struggles becoming weaker.

Reese stumbled against the back steps, then up onto
the porch. The house blocked some of the wind, and
he managed to open the back door, then reach up and
unhook both their lines. He staggered into the house
and fell to the floor of the utility room with Madelyn
still in his arms, but managed to turn so that he took
most of the shock. "Are you all right?" He gasped the
question, breathing hard from exertion. The wind had
gotten worse just since he'd made it back to the barn.

She didn't answer, and sudden fear brought him up on his knees beside her. Her eyes were closed, her lips blue. He grabbed her shoulder, shouting at her. "Maddie! Madelyn, damn it, what's wrong? Are you hurt—wake up and answer me!"

She coughed, then moaned a little and tried to curl on her side, her arms coming up to hug herself. She coughed again, then went into a paroxysm of convulsive coughing and gagging, writhing from the force of it. Reese pulled her up into his arms and held her, his face white.

Finally she managed to wheeze, "Shut the door," and he lashed out with his boot, kicking the door shut with a force that rattled it on its frame.

He unwound the scarf from her head and began opening her coat. The rope around their waists still tied them together and he hastily pulled the knots out. "Are you hurt?" he asked again, his face a grim mask.

Coughing had brought color to her face, but it was quickly fading, leaving her deathly pale. "I'm all right," she said, her voice so hoarse she could barely make a sound. "I just couldn't breathe."

Realization hit him like a kick by a mule. He'd almost smothered her with the force of his grip. His face grim, vicious curses coming from between his tightly clenched teeth, he laid her back on the floor as gently as possible and stretched out his leg so he could get his knife out of his pocket. Her eyes widened as he snapped the blade open and began slicing through the pullover sweater she wore under the coat. Beneath the sweater was a shirt, but it buttoned down the front and therefore escaped being cut off. When her torso was bare he bagan carefully feeling her ribs, his face intent as he searched for any sign of give, his eyes locked on her face to see the least hint of discomfort. She flinched several times, but the ribs felt all right. Her pale skin was already becoming discolored with bruises.

"I almost killed you," he said harshly as he lifted her in his arms and got to his feet.

"It wasn't that bad," she managed to say.

He gave her a violent look. "You were unconscious." He carried her up the stairs and to their bedroom, where he laid her on the bed. He shrugged out of his own coat and let it fall to the floor; then he very gently but implacably stripped her of every stitch and examined her from head to toe. Except for the bruising across her ribs, she was fine. He bent his head and brushed his lips across the dark band as if he would absorb the pain.

Madelyn put her hand on his hair, threading her fingers through the dark strands. "Reese, I'm okay, I promise."

He got to his feet. "I'll put a cold compress on it to stop the bruising from getting any worse."

She made a disbelieving sound. "Trust me, I can't just lie here and let you put an ice bag on my side! You know how ice down your shirt feels, and besides, I'm cold. I'd rather have a cup of hot chocolate, or coffee."

The strength of her tone reassured him, and another critical look told him that the color was coming back into her face. She sat up, rather gingerly holding her side but without any real pain, and gave him a wifely survey. "You're soaking wet from riding in that blizzard. You need to get out of those clothes, and then we'll both have something hot to drink.''

She got dry clothes out for both Reese and herself and began dressing while he stripped and toweled off. She looked at her ruined sweater with disbelief, then tossed it into the trash. Reese saw her expression and smiled faintly. ''I didn't want to move you any more than I had to until I knew what was wrong,'' he explained, rubbing a towel over his shoulders.

''Actually, I was a little relieved when the sweater was all you cut. For a split second I was afraid you were going to do a tracheotomy.''

''You were talking and breathing, so I ruled that out. I've done one before, though.''

''You've actually taken your pocketknife and cut someone's throat open?'' she demanded incredulously, her voice rising.

''I had to. One of the hands got kicked in the throat, and he was choking to death. I slit his trachea and held it open with my finger until someone brought a drinking straw to insert for him to breathe through. We got him to a hospital, they put in a regular trach tube until the swelling went down enough for him to breathe again, and he did just fine.''

''How did you know what to do?''

''Every rancher absorbs a lot of medical knowledge just in the ordinary workday. I've set broken bones, sewn up cuts, given injections. It's a rough life, sweetheart.'' His face darkened as he said it. It had almost been too rough for her. He could so easily have crushed her ribs.

He pulled on the dry underwear and jeans she had put out for him, watching as she brushed her hair and swung it back over her shoulder with a practiced toss of her head, every movement as graceful as a ballet. How could she still look elegant after what she'd been through? How could she be so casual about it? He was still shaking.

When she started past him on the way downstairs, he caught her and wrapped his arms around her, holding her to him for a long minute with his cheek resting on top of her pale hair. Madelyn circled his waist with her arms and let herself revel in his closeness; he was home, and he was all right. Nothing was said, because nothing needed saying. It was enough just to hold each other.

Reese paced the house that day like a restless cougar, periodically looking out the window to monitor the weather. He tried a radio station, but nothing came through the static. Around dusk the electricity went off, and he built a roaring fire in the fireplace, then put one of the kerosene heaters in the kitchen. Madelyn lit candles and lamps, and thanked the stars that the water heater and stove were gas-operated.

They ate soup and sandwiches by candlelight, then brought down quilts and blankets and pillows to sleep in front of the fireplace. They sat on their bed of quilts with their backs resting against the front of the couch and their legs stretched toward the fire. Madelyn's head was on his shoulder. He could almost hear her mind working as she stared at the fire, and he decided he might as well get it started before she did. "A flag with a swallow-tail end is called a burgee."

She gave him a quick look of delight. "The small flag carried in front or to the right of marchers to guide them is called a guidon."

"You want to do flags? Okay, we'll do flags. The study of flags is called vexillology."

"The United States flag has seven red stripes and six white."

"That one's so easy it's cheating."

"A fact is a fact. Carry on."

"Bamboo is the fastest growing plant in the world."

"Cleopatra was Macedonian, not Egyptian."

They played the game for several more minutes, laughing at the more ridiculous items they pulled out. Then they got a deck of cards and played strip poker, which wasn't much of a challenge, since she was wearing only his shirt and a pair of socks, and he was wearing only jeans. Once she had him naked, she lost interest in playing cards and moved on to a more rewarding occupation. With flame-burnished skin they moved together and for a long while forgot about the swirling white storm that enveloped them.

The blizzard conditions had subsided by the next morning, though deep drifts had been piled up by the wind. The electricity came back on, and the weather report predicted slowly moderating temperatures. Reese checked on the herd and found that the cattle had withstood the storm in good condition; he lost only one calf, which had gotten lost from its mother. He found the little animal lying in a snowbank, while its mother bawled mournfully, calling it.

They had been lucky this time. He looked up at the gray sky, where patches of blue were just starting to show through. All he needed was a mild winter, or at least one where the bad spells didn't last long enough to endanger the herd.

He was pulling his way out of the morass of debt, but one year of profit was a long way from being home free. He needed the mortgage paid off, he needed an expanded herd and the money to hire cowhands to work that herd. When he could expand his capital into other areas so he wasn't entirely dependent on the weather and the market for beef, then he would feel more secure about their future.

The next few years wouldn't be easy. Madelyn wasn't pregnant yet, but as soon as she was they would have medical bills to consider, as well as the cost of providing for a growing baby. Maybe he should take Robert's offer despite his disinclination to allow anyone else any authority over the ranch. It would give him a financial cushion, the means of putting his plans into operation sooner, as well as taking care of Madelyn and their child, or children.

But he had been through too much, fought too hard and too long, to change his mind now. The ranch was his, as much a part of him as bone and blood.

He could easier lose his own life than the ranch. He loved every foot of it with the same fierce, independent possessiveness that had kept his ancestors there despite Indian attacks, weather and disease. Reese had grown up with the sun on his face and the scent of cattle in his nostrils, as much a part of this land as the purple-tinged mountains and enormous sky.

"I'll make it yet," he said aloud to the white, silent land. It wasn't in him to give up, but the land had required men like him from the beginning. It had broken weaker men, and the ones who had survived were tougher and stronger than most. The land had needed strong women, too, and if Madelyn wasn't quite what he'd planned on, he was too satisfied to care.

9

At the end of January another big weather system began moving in from the Arctic, and this one looked bad. They had a couple of days' warning, and they worked together to do everything they could to safeguard the herd. The cold front moved in during the night, and they woke the next morning to steady snow and a temperature that was ten below zero, but at least the wind wasn't as bad as it had been before.

Reese made a couple of forays out to break the ice in the troughs and stock ponds so the cattle could drink, and Madelyn was terrified every time he went out. This kind of cold was the killing kind, and the weather reports said it would get worse.

It did. The temperature dropped all that day, and by nightfall it was twenty-three below zero.

When morning came it was forty-one degrees below zero, and the wind was blowing.

If Reese had been restless before, he was like a caged animal now. They wore layers of clothing even in the house, and he kept a fire in the fireplace even though the electricity was still on. They constantly drank hot coffee or chocolate to keep their temperatures up, and they moved down to the living room to sleep before the fire.

The third day he just sat, his eyes black with inner rage. His cattle were dying out there, and he was helpless to do a damn thing about it; the blowing snow kept him from getting to them. The killing temperatures would kill him even faster than they would the cattle. The wind chill was seventy below zero.

Lying before the fire that night, Madelyn put her hand on his chest and felt the tautness of his body. His eyes were open, and he was staring at the ceiling. She rose up on her elbow. "No matter what happens," she said quietly, "we'll make it."

His voice was harsh. "We can't make it without the cattle."

"Then you're just giving up?"

The look he gave her was violent. He didn't know how to give up; the words were obscene to him.

"We'll work harder," she said. "Last spring you didn't have me here to help you. We'll be able to do more."

His face softened, and he lifted her hand in his, holding it up in the firelight and studying it, slim and femininely graceful. She was willing to turn her hands to any job, no matter how rough or dirty, so he didn't have the heart to tell her that whenever she was with him, he was so concerned for her safety that he spent most of his time watching after her. She wouldn't understand it; they had been married for seven months, and she hadn't backed down from anything that had been thrown at her. She certainly hadn't backed down from him. Remembering some of their fights made him smile, and remembering others made him get hard. It hadn't been a dull seven months.

"You're right," he said, holding her hand to his face. "We'll just work harder."

It was the fourth day before they could get out. The wind had died, and the sky was a clear blue bowl, making a mockery of the bitter cold. They had to wrap their faces to even breathe, it was so cold, and it taxed their endurance just to get to the barn to care for the animals there. The cow was in abject misery, her udder so swollen and sore she kicked every time Reese tried to milk her. It took over an hour of starts and stops before she would stand still and let him finish the job. Madelyn took care of the horses while he attended to the milking, carrying water and feed, and then shoveling out the stalls and putting down fresh straw.

The animals seemed nervous and glad to see them; tears stung her eyes as she rubbed Reese's favorite mount on the forehead. These animals had had the protection of the barn; she couldn't bear to even think about the cattle.

Reese got the truck started and loaded it and a small trailer with hay. Madelyn climbed into the cab and gave him a steady look when he frowned at her. There was no way she would let him go out on the range by himself in such bitter cold; if anything happened to him, if he fell and couldn't get back to the truck or lost consciousness, he would die in a short while.

He drove carefully to the protected area where he had herded the cattle and stopped, his face bleak. There was nothing there, just a blank white landscape. The sun glittered on the snow, and he reached for his sunglasses. Without a word Madelyn followed suit.

He began driving, looking for any sign of the herd, if indeed any of them had survived. That white blanket could be covering their frozen carcasses.

Finally it was the pitiful bawling that led them to some of the cattle. They had gone in search of food, or perhaps more shelter, but they were in a stand of trees where the snow had blown an enormous snowbank up against the tree trunks, blocking some of the wind and perhaps saving them.

Reese's face was still shuttered as he got out to toss some bales of hay down from the trailer, and Madelyn knew how he felt. He was afraid to hope, afraid that only a few head had survived. He cut the twine on the bales and loosened the hay, then took a shovel and dug an opening in the snowbank. The anxious cattle crowded out of what had become a pen to them and headed for the hay. Reese counted them, and his face tightened. Madelyn could tell that this was only a fraction of the number there should have been.

He got back into the truck and sat with his gloved hands clenched on the steering wheel.

"If these survived, there could be more," Madelyn said. "We have to keep looking."

By a frozen pond they found more, but these were lying on their sides in pathetic, snow-covered humps. Reese counted again. Thirty-six were dead, and there could be calves too small to find under all the snow.

One cow had become trapped in a tangle of brush and wire, and her calf was lying on the snow beside her, watching with innocent brown eyes as its mother weakly struggled. Reese cut her free, and she scrambled to her feet, but then was too weak to do anything else. The calf got up too, stumbling on shaky legs to seek her milk. Reese put out hay for her to eat and continued the search for more.

They found seven survivors in a gully, and ten more carcasses not five hundred feet away. That was how it went for the rest of the day: as many as they found alive, they found that many dead. He put out hay, used an axe to chop holes in the ice-covered ponds, and kept a tally of both his losses and the ones that had survived. Half of the herd was dead, and more could die. The grimness of the situation weighed down on him. He'd been so close—and now this!

The next day they rounded up the strays, trying to get the herd together. Reese rode, and Madelyn drove the truck, pulling another trailer of hay. The temperature was moderating, if you could call ten below zero moderate, but it was too late.

One yearling objected to rejoining the herd and darted to the left, with the horse immediately following suit and getting in front of the impetuous young animal, herding it back the way it had come. The young bull stubbornly stopped, its head swinging back and forth, looking for all the world like a recalcitrant teenager. Then it made another break for freedom and bolted across a pond, but it was a pond where Reese had chopped holes in the ice near the bank, and it hadn't refrozen solid enough to hold the yearling's weight, which was already considerable. Its rear feet broke through, and it fell backward, great eyes rolling while it bawled in terror.

Cussing a blue streak, Reese got his rope and approached the bank. Madelyn pulled the truck up and got out. "Don't go out on the ice," she warned.

"Don't worry, I'm not as stupid as he is," he muttered, shaking loose a loop and twirling it a few times. He missed the first throw because the young bull was struggling frantically, and its struggles were breaking off more ice; it slipped backward and went completely under the icy water just as Reese made his throw. Still swearing, he quickly recoiled the rope as Madelyn joined him.

The second throw settled neatly around the tossing head, and Reese quickly wound the rope around the saddle horn. The horse began backing up under his quiet instructions and the pressure of his hand, dragging the yearling from the water.

As soon as the yearling was free of the water the horse stopped and Reese kept his hand on the rope as he worked to loosen the loop around the bull's neck. As soon as it was free, the animal gave a panicked bawl and bolted into Reese, its muscled shoulder knocking him sideways into the water.

Madelyn bit back a scream as she ran forward, waiting for him to surface. He did, only about ten feet out, but they were ten feet he couldn't negotiate. The numbing cold of the water was almost immediately paralyzing. All he could do was drape his arms over the edge of the broken ice and hang on.

She grabbed the rope and urged the horse forward, but she couldn't swing a loop and in any case wouldn't drag him out by his neck. "Can you catch the rope?" she called urgently, and one gloved hand moved in what she hoped was an affirmative answer. She slung the rope across the water toward him, and he made an effort to raise his arm and catch it, but his movement was slow and clumsy, and the rope fell into the water.

She had to get him out of there *now*. Two minutes from now might be too late. Her heart was slamming against her rib cage, and her face was paper-white. There was no help for him except herself, and no time for indecision. She pulled the rope back to her and ran to the pond, edging out on the ice herself.

He raised his head, his eyes filling with horror as he saw her inching toward him. "No!" he said hoarsely.

She went down on her belly and began snaking toward him, distributing her weight over as much of the ice as she could, but even so she felt it cracking beneath her. Ten feet. Just ten feet. It sounded so close in theory, and in practice it was forever.

The edge of the ice he'd been holding crumbled, and he went under. She scrambled forward, forsaking safety for speed. Just as he broke the surface again she grabbed the collar of his coat and pulled him upward; the combined pressure of their weight caused more ice to fracture and she almost fell in with him but she scrambled back just enough.

"I have the rope," she said, her teeth chattering in terror. "I'm going to slip it over your head and under your arms. Then the horse will drag you out. Okay?"

He nodded. His lips were blue, but he managed to raise one arm at a time so she could get the rope on him. She leaned forward to tighten the slip knot, and the ice beneath her gave with a sharp crack, dropping her straight downward.

Cold. She had never known such cold. It took her breath, and her limbs immediately went numb. Her eyes were open, and she saw her hair float in front of her face. She was under the water. Odd that it didn't matter. Up above she could see a white blanket with

dark spots in it, and a strange disturbance.
Reese . . . maybe it was Reese.

The thought of Reese was what focused her splin-
tered thoughts. Somehow she managed to begin flail-
ing her arms and legs, fighting her way to the surface,
aiming for one of those dark spots that represented
breaks in the ice.

Her face broke the surface just as the horse, working on its own, hauled Reese up on the bank. It was
trained to pull when it felt weight on the end of the
rope, so it had. She reached for the edge of the ice as
Reese struggled to his hands and knees.

"Maddie!" His voice was a hoarse cry as he fought
to free himself of the rope, his coordination almost
gone.

Hold on. All she had to do was hold on. It was what
she had been praying he would be able to do, and now
it was what she had to do. She tried, but she didn't
have his strength. Her weight began dragging her
down, and she couldn't stop it. The water closed over
her head again.

She had to fight upward, had to swim. Her thoughts
were sluggish, but they directed her movements
enough so that just when she thought her tortured
lungs would give out and she would have to inhale, she
broke through to the surface again.

"Grab the ice. Maddie, grab the ice!" He barked
out the command in a tone of voice that made her
reach outward in a blind motion, one that by chance
laid her arm across the ice.

The wet rope was freezing, making it stiff. Reese
fought the cold, fought his own clumsiness as he
swung the loop. "Hold your other arm up so I can get

the loop over it. Maddie, hold—your—other—arm—
up!''

She couldn't. She had already been in the water too
long. All she could do was lift the arm that had been
holding on to the ice and hope that he could snare it
before she went completely under.

He swung the loop out as her face disappeared under the water. It settled around her outstretched arm,
and with a frantic jerk he tightened it, the loop
shrinking to almost nothing as it closed around her
slender wrist. "Back, back!" he yelled at the horse,
which was already bracing itself against the weight it
could feel.

She was dragged underwater toward the bank, and
finally up on it. Reese fell to his knees beside her,
screaming hell in his eyes until she began choking and
retching. "We'll be all right," he said fiercely as he
fumbled with the slip knot around her wrist, trying to
free her. "All we have to do is get to the house and
we'll be all right." He didn't even let himself think that
they might not make it. Even though they weren't that
far, it would take all his strength.

He was too cold to lift her, so he dragged her to
the truck. Her eyes kept closing. "Don't go to sleep,"
he said harshly. "Open your eyes. Fight, damn it!
Fight!"

Her gray eyes opened, but there was no real com-
prehension in them. To his astonishment, her fist
doubled, and she tried to swing at him as she obeyed
his rough command.

He got the truck door open and half boosted, half
pushed her up onto the seat. She sprawled across it,
dripping water.

The horse nudged him. If the animal hadn't been so close he would have left it behind, but a lifetime of taking care of his livestock prompted him to tie the reins to the rear bumper. He wouldn't be able to drive so fast that the horse couldn't easily keep pace, even though every instinct screamed that he had to get to the house and get both of them warm.

He pulled himself onto the seat behind the steering wheel and turned on the ignition, then struggled to slide the knob that turned the heater on high. Hot air poured out of the vents, but he was too numb to feel it.

They had to get out of their clothes. The icy wetness was just leaching more heat away from their bodies. He began fighting out of his coat as he barked orders at Madelyn to do the same.

She managed to sit up somehow, but she had almost no coordination. She had been in the water even longer than he had. He didn't have an easy time of it, but by the time he was naked she was weakly pushing her heavy shearling coat onto the floorboard. Ice crystals had already caked it.

He reached for her buttons. "Come on, sweetheart, we have to get you naked. The clothes will just make you that much colder. Can you talk to me? Say something, Maddie. Talk to me."

She slowly lifted one hand, with all the fingers folded down except the middle one. He looked at the obscene, or suggestive, gesture—it all depended on how he took it—and despite the gravity of the situation a rough laugh burst from his throat. "I'll take you up on that, sweetheart, just as soon as we get warm." A sparkle came into her eyes, giving him hope.

His teeth began chattering, and convulsive shudders racked him. Maddie wasn't shivering, and that was a bad sign. There were always a blanket and a thermos of coffee in the truck when he went out in the winter, and he pulled the blanket out from behind the seat. Even the simplest movement was a battle requiring all his strength, but he finally got it out and roughly dried them with it as best he could, then wrapped it around her.

With shaking hands he opened the thermos and poured a small amount of steaming coffee into the top, then held it to her lips. "Drink, baby. It's nice and hot."

She managed to swallow a little of it, and he drank the rest himself, then poured more into the cup. He could feel it burning down into his stomach. If he didn't get himself into shape to drive to the ranch, neither one of them would make it. He fought the shaking of his hands until he had downed the entire cup, then poured more and coaxed Madelyn into taking it. That was all he could do for now. He focused his attention and put the truck in gear.

It was slow going. He was shaking so hard that his body wouldn't obey. He was a little disoriented, sometimes unable to tell where they were. Beside him, Madelyn finally began shivering as the heat blasting from the vents combined with the coffee to revive her a little.

The house had never looked so good to him as it did when it finally came into view and he nursed the truck across the rough ground toward it. He parked as close to the back door as possible and walked naked around the truck to haul Madelyn out the passenger door. He couldn't feel the snow under his bare feet.

She could walk a little now, and that helped. With their arms around each other they half crawled up the steps to the porch, then into the utility room. The downstairs bathroom was directly across from the utility room; he dragged Madelyn into it and propped her against the wall while he turned on the water in the tub to let it get hot. When steam began rising he turned the cold water tap and hoped he adjusted it right, or they would be scalded. His hands were so cold he simply couldn't tell.

"Come on, into the tub."

She struggled to her knees, and Reese pulled her up the rest of the way, but in the end it was simpler for both of them to literally crawl over the edge of the tub into the rising water. She sat in front of him and between his legs, lying back against his chest. Tears ran down her face as the warm water lapped against her cold flesh, bringing it painfully back to life. Reese let his head tilt back until it rested on the wall, his teeth gritted. They had to endure it because it was necessary; they didn't have anyone else here to take care of them. This was the fastest way to get warm, but it wasn't pleasant.

Slowly the pain in their extremities eased. When the water was so high that it was lapping out the overflow drain, he turned off the tap and sank deeper until his shoulders were covered. Madelyn's hair floated on the surface like wet gold.

He tightened his arms around her, trying to absorb her shivering into him.

"Better?"

"Yes." Her voice was low and even huskier than usual. "That was close."

He turned her in his arms and hugged her to him with barely controlled desperation. "I was planning to keep that bull for breeding," he said tightly, "but the sonofabitch is going to be a steer now—if he lives through this."

She managed a laugh, her lips moving against his throat. The water lapped her chin. "Don't ever get rid of that horse. He saved our bacon."

"I'll give him the biggest stall for the rest of his life."

They lay in the water until it began to cool; then he pulled the plug and urged her to her feet. She was still looking sleepy, so he held her to him while he closed the shower curtain and turned on the shower, letting the water beat down on their heads. She just stood in his arms with her head on his chest, the way she had stood so many times, but this time was infinitely precious. This time they had cheated death.

The water rained over them. He turned her face up and took her mouth, needing her taste, her touch, to reassure himself that they were really okay. He had come incredibly close to losing her, even closer than he had come to dying himself.

When the hot water began to go he snapped off the tap and reached for towels, wrapping one around her dripping hair and using another to dry her. Though her lips and nails had color now, she was still shivering a little, and he supported her as she stepped carefully from the tub. He took another towel and began rubbing his own head, all the while watching every move she made.

Madelyn felt warm, but incredibly lethargic. She had no more energy than if she had been recovering from a monster case of the flu. More than anything she wanted to lie down in front of the fire and sleep for a week, but she knew enough about hypothermia to be afraid to. She sat on the toilet seat and watched him towel dry, focusing on the magnificent strength made more evident by his nakedness. He gave her a reason to fight her lethargy now, just as he had when she had been on the bottom of the pond.

He cupped her face, making certain she was paying attention. "Don't go to sleep," he warned. "Stay in here where it's hot while I go upstairs to get your robe. Okay?"

She nodded. "Okay."

"I won't be but a minute."

She managed a smile, just to reassure him. "Bring my brush and comb, too."

It took several minutes, but he came back with her robe toasty warm from the clothes dryer, and she shuddered with pleasure as he wrapped it around her. He had taken the time to almost dress, too; he had on socks, unsnapped jeans and a flannel shirt left unbuttoned. He had brought socks for her, and he knelt to slip them on her feet.

He kept his arm around her waist as they went into the kitchen. He pulled out a chair and placed her in it. "Open your mouth," he said, and when she did he slid the thermometer, which he'd brought from the upstairs bathroom, under her tongue. "Now sit there and be still while I make a pot of coffee."

That wasn't hard to do. The only thing she wanted to do more than sit still was to lie down.

When the digital thermometer twittered its alarm, he pulled it out of her mouth and frowned at it. "Ninety six point four. I want it up at least another degree."

"What about you?"

"I'm more alert than you are. I'm bigger, and I wasn't in the water as long." He could still feel a deep inner chill, but nothing like the bone-numbing cold he had felt before. The first cup of coffee almost completely dispelled the rest of the coldness, as both the heat and the caffeine did their work. He made Madelyn drink three cups of coffee, even though she had revived enough to caustically point out that, as usual, he'd made it so strong she was likely to go into caffeine overdose. He watered it down for her, his mouth wry.

When he felt safer about leaving her, he deposited her on the quilts in front of the fire. "I have to go back out," he said, and he saw panic flare in her eyes. "Not to the range," he added quickly. "I have to put the horse back in the barn and take care of him. I'll be back as soon as I'm finished."

"I'm not going anywhere," she reassured him.

She was still afraid to lie down and go to sleep, even though so much caffeine was humming through her system that she wasn't certain she would be able to go to sleep that night. She pulled the towel off her head and began combing the tangles out of her hair.

By the time he got back, her hair was dry and she was brushing it into order. He stopped in the doorway, struck as always by the intensely female beauty of the ritual. Her sleeves dropped away from her arms as she lifted them, revealing pale, slender forearms.

Her neck was gracefully bent, like a flower nodding in the breeze. His throat tightened, and blood rushed to his loins as he watched her; seven months of marriage and he was still reacting to her like a stallion scenting a mare.

"How are you feeling?" The words were raspy. He had to force them out.

She looked up, her slow smile heating his blood even more. "Better. Warm and awake. How are *you* after going back out into the cold?"

"I'm okay." More than okay. They were both alive, and there wasn't a cell in his body that was cold.

He insisted on taking her temperature again and waited impatiently until the thermometer twittered. "Ninety-seven point six. Good."

"My normal temperature isn't much more than that. It usually hovers in the low ninety-eights."

"Mine is usually around ninety-nine or a little higher."

"I'm not surprised. Sleeping with you is like sleeping with a furnace."

"Complaining?"

She shook her head. "Bragging." Her smile faded, and her gray eyes darkened to charcoal as she reached out to touch his face. "I almost lost you." He saw the flash of sheer terror in her eyes just before she closed them, and he grabbed her to him with almost desperate relief.

"Baby, I came a lot closer to losing you than you did to losing me," he said roughly, moving his lips against her hair.

Madelyn wound her arms around his neck. She didn't often cry; her moods were too even and generally upbeat. The two times she had cried since their marriage had both been the result of pain, once on their wedding night and again just an hour before when the warm water in the tub had begun bringing life back into her frozen skin. But suddenly the enormity and strain of what they had been through swept over her, and her chest tightened. She tried to fight it, tried to keep her composure, but it was a losing battle. With a wrenching sob she buried her face against his throat and clung to him while her body shook with the force of her weeping.

He was more than surprised by her sudden tears, he was astounded. His Maddie was a fighter, one who met his strength with her own and didn't flinch even from his worst tempers. But now she was sobbing as if she would never stop, and the depth of her distress punched him in the chest. He crooned to her and rubbed her back, whispering reassurances as he lowered her to the quilts.

It took a long time for her sobs to quiet. He didn't try to get her to stop, sensing that she needed the release, just as he had needed the release of savagely kicking a feed bucket the length of the barn after he had taken care of his horse. He just held her until the storm was over, then gave her his handkerchief for mopping up.

Her eyelids were swollen, and she looked exhausted, but there was no more tightly wound tension in her eyes as she lay quietly in the aftermath. Reese propped himself up on an elbow and tugged at the belt of her robe, pulling it loose and then spreading the lapels to expose her nude body.

He trailed his fingers across the hollow of her throat, then over to her slender collarbone. "Have I ever told you," he asked musingly, "that just looking at you gets me so hard it hurts?"

Her voice was husky. "No, but you've demonstrated it a few times."

"It does hurt. I feel like I'm going to explode. Then, when I get inside you, the hurt changes to pleasure." He stroked his hand down to her breast, covering it with the warmth of his palm and feeling her nipple softly pushing at him. Gently he caressed her, circling the nipple with his thumb until it stood upright and darkened in color; then he bent over her to kiss the enticing little nub. Her breathing had changed, getting deeper, and a delicate flush was warming her skin. When he looked up he saw how heavy-lidded her eyes had become, and he was flooded with fiercely masculine satisfaction that he could make her look like that.

Once he had tried to deny himself the sensual pleasure of feasting on her, but no longer. He let himself be absorbed as he stroked his hand down her body, savoring the silky texture of her skin, shaping his hand to the curves and indentations that flowed from one to the other, the swell of her breast to the flat of her stomach, the flare of her hips, the notch between her legs. He watched his tanned, powerful fingers slide through the little triangle of curls and then probe between her soft folds, fascinated by the contrast between his hand and her pale feminine body.

And the taste of her. There was the heated sweetness of her mouth; he sampled it, then tasted again more deeply, making love to her with his tongue. Then there was the warm, fragrant hollow of her throat, and the rose-and-milk taste of her breasts. He lingered there for a long time, until her hands were knotting and twisting in the quilt, and her hips were lifting against him.

Her belly was cool against his lips, and silky smooth. Her tight little navel invited exploration, and he circled it with his tongue. Her hands moved into his hair and tightly pressed against his skull as he moved downward, parting her thighs and draping them over his shoulders.

She was breathing hard, her body twisting and straining. He held her hips and loved her, not stopping until she heaved upward and cried out as the waves of completion overtook her.

She felt drained, more exhausted than before. She lay limply as he knelt between her legs and tore at his clothes, throwing them aside. She could barely open her eyes as he positioned himself and then invaded her with a slow, heavy thrust that carried him into her to the hilt. As always, she was faintly startled by the overwhelming sense of fullness as she adjusted to him.

His full weight was on her, crushing her downward. There was nothing gentlemanly about him now, only the need to enter her as deeply as possible, to carry the embrace to the fullest so that there was no part of her that didn't feel his possession. His lovemaking was often dominant, but she could usually meet it with her own strength. She couldn't now; there was a savagery in him that had to be appeased, a hunger that had to be fed. Even though he restrained himself so that he never hurt her, she was helpless to do anything but lie there and accept him, and feel her passion rising within her again with a beating rhythm.

He paused when his tension reached the critical level, not wanting it to end just yet. His green eyes glittered as he framed her face in his hands and measured the strength of her arousal.

He brushed his mouth against her ear. "Did you know that a man normally has..."

She listened to the words rustling in her ear, her hands tightening on his back as she struggled for control. Though she loved their trivia game, she wasn't in the mood for it now. Finally she gasped, "I wonder why there are so many, when one will do."

In his best big-bad-wolf voice, admittedly ragged, he said, "The better to get you pregnant, my dear," and he began moving again, hard and fast. And, sometime within the next hour, he did.

10

Reese went over the figures again, but the totals didn't change. He got to his feet and looked out the window, his hands knotted into fists and his jaw set. All those years of work. All those *damn* years of work, for nothing.

He had done everything he could think of, cut down on every expense until there was nothing left that could be cut, and still those figures spelled it out in black and white: he had lost. The January blizzard that had killed half of his herd had pushed him so far under that the bank couldn't carry him any longer. He couldn't make the mortgage, and there would be no more extensions.

He had three options: one, he could let the bank foreclose, and they would lose everything; two, he could file chapter eleven bankruptcy and keep the ranch but ruin his credit; and three, he could accept Robert's offer to be an investor. He smiled grimly. Number three was an option only if Robert's offer was still open, considering that he had made it when the ranch was profitable and now it was going under fast.

He had been so close to making it. He thought that was what made the final defeat so bitter, that he had been close enough to see the end of debt. What April had started almost eight years before was finally coming to fruition: the destruction of his ranch. Who knew what her reasoning had been? Maybe she had done it because he had loved the ranch so much, more than he had ever even thought he loved her. It was his lifeblood, and he was losing it, unless Robert Cannon still wanted to invest. Reese went over the options again, but Robert was his only chance, and a slim one at that, because when Robert saw the figures he would have to be a hell of a gambler to go through with the deal. Reese didn't hold out much hope, but he would make the effort, because he couldn't do otherwise. He didn't have just himself to consider now; he had Madelyn, and he would do what he could to keep her home for her. She hadn't married him expecting bankruptcy or foreclosure.

It was March; snow was still on the ground, but the throbbing promise of spring was in the air. In another week or so buds would begin to swell on the trees and bushes; the land was alive, but the taste of ashes was in his mouth, because this might be the last spring he would ever see on his ranch.

He could hear Maddie in the kitchen, humming along with the radio as she gathered the ingredients for baking a cake. She'd gotten good at baking, so good that his mouth began watering every time those warm smells drifted his way. She was happy here. He hadn't married her expecting anything more than a work partner, but instead he'd gotten a warm, intelligent, amusing and sexy woman who loved him. She never seemed embarrassed about it, never tried to pressure him into giving her more than he could; she simply loved him and didn't try to hide it.

He didn't know how he would tell her, but she had a right to know.

She was licking cake batter from a wooden spoon when he walked in, and she gave him a wink as she held the spoon out. "Wanna lick?"

The batter was on her fingers, too. He started at her fingers and worked his way up the handle of the spoon, his tongue scooping up the sweet batter. When the spoon was clean he turned to her fingers to make certain he'd gotten it all. "Any more?"

She produced the bowl and swiped her finger around the edge, then popped it in her mouth laden with batter. "Your turn."

They cleaned the bowl like two children. That was probably Maddie's most endearing trait, the ease with which she found enjoyment in life, and she had taught him how to have fun again. It was just simple things, like their trivia game or licking a bowl, but he had lost the knack for having fun until she had entered his life and taken over.

He hated having to tell her that they might lose their home. A man was supposed to take care of his wife. Maybe that was old-fashioned and chauvinistic, but that was the way he felt. It ate at his pride like acid not to be able to provide for her.

He sighed and put his hands on her waist, his face grim. "We have to talk."

She eyed him cautiously. "I've never liked conversations that begin with that phrase."

"You won't like this one, either. It's serious."

She searched his face, her eyes becoming somber as she read his expression. "What is it?"

"When we lost half the herd, it put us under. I can't make the mortgage." That was it in a nutshell, as succinct and bald as he could make it.

"Can we get an extension—"

"No. If I had the full herd as collateral, then it would be possible, but I don't have enough beef on the hoof to cover the outstanding debt."

"Robert said you have the best head for business he's ever seen. What do we have to do, and what can we do?"

He outlined the three things that could happen, and she listened to him with an intent expression. When he had finished she asked, "Why don't you think Robert's offer would still stand?"

"Because the ranch is a losing proposition now."

"You're still here, and it was you he was willing to bet on, not X number of cows." Then she said, "There's another option you haven't mentioned."

"What's that?"

"I told you before, I have some money—"

He dropped his hands. "No. I've told *you* before."

"Why not?" she asked calmly.

"I've told you that before, too. It hasn't changed."

"Do you mean you'd actually give up the ranch before you would let me put my money in it?"

His eyes looked like flint. "Yes, that's exactly what I mean." Maddie had changed a lot of his attitudes, but that one was still intact and as strong as ever. A business partner was one thing, because rights were limited by contract. A marriage was something else, subject to the whims of a judge with little regard to fairness. April had proved that to him.

Madelyn turned away before her expression betrayed her. Not for anything would she let him see how that hurt her. With perfect control she said, "It's your ranch, your decision."

"Exactly, and it will stay my ranch, my decision, until the day I get thrown off."

Her mind was busy as she cooked dinner, and determination grew in her. If he thought she would stand by and see the ranch go under when she had the means to save it, he would learn differently. She didn't know how much the mortgage was, and she had told him the truth when she'd said that her trust fund was far from being a fortune, but surely it was enough to buy them some time until the ranch was on a firmer footing.

He'd never said he loved her. Maybe he didn't, but Madelyn thought he was at least fond of her. He certainly desired her, though it was true that a man could physically desire a woman without caring for her as a person. If he had lived with her for nine months and still thought she was capable of doing the sort of thing April had done, then perhaps he didn't care for her as much as she'd thought. She had been happy, but now her balloon was fast going flat.

Now wasn't the time to tell him she was pregnant. Or maybe it was. Maybe knowing about the baby would bring him to his senses, reassure him that she wasn't going anywhere, and that they had to use whatever means were at their disposal to save their child's inheritance.

But she didn't tell him. His mood varied from taciturn to biting sarcasm, the way it did when he was angry, and she didn't feel like prodding him into a full-scale blowup. Though she was only two months along, she was already beginning to feel the effects of pregnancy in lower energy levels and a slightly upset stomach—not the best time to battle with her husband.

He was still in a bad mood when he left the next morning, and he took a lunch with him, which meant he wouldn't be back until it was time for dinner. Madelyn hesitated for maybe five minutes.

She didn't like going behind his back, but if that was the way it had to be, then she would face the music later. It was a long drive to Billings; she might not make it back before he did, but that was another bridge she would cross when she came to it. While she was there she would also phone around for an obstetrician, because there wasn't any sort of doctor in Crook, and she didn't know of one any closer than Billings. It could get interesting around her delivery time, she thought, with her doctor a three-hour drive away.

She hastily dressed, got her checkbook and the necessary documents, and ran out to the car. It had snow tires on it if she needed them, but the highways were clear, so she hoped she would make good time.

She drove quickly but carefully, thankful that there wasn't much traffic to contend with, and reached the bank at eleven-thirty. She knew who Reese dealt with, having accompanied him before, and she only had to wait about fifteen minutes before the man could see her.

He was smiling the way bankers do, his hand outstretched. "Good morning, Mrs. Duncan. What can we do for you?"

"Good morning, Mr. VanRoden. I'd like to know the amount of our outstanding mortgage."

He stroked his upper lip as if he had a mustache, which he didn't, and looked thoughtful. "Well, I'm not certain I can tell you. You see, the mortgage is only in your husband's name."

She didn't bother trying to argue with bureaucracy or banking rules and went straight to the point. "If it's under two hundred thousand dollars, I want to pay it off."

There was nothing that got a banker's attention like money. He chewed his lip, studying her. She sat very calmly and let him try to pick up what clues he could from her appearance, though she had deliberately dressed that morning in one of her New York suits and twisted her hair up. If he could read anything in a charcoal suit with a pink silk blouse under it and an iridescent peacock pinned to the lapel, he was welcome to draw any conclusions he could.

He made up his mind with a minimum of dithering. "Let me check the file," he said. "I'll be right back."

She waited, certain of the outcome. No bank would refuse the repayment of a loan, regardless of who was doing the paying. She supposed a rank stranger could walk in off the street and pay off any loan he chose, as long as he had the means to do it.

VanRoden was back in less than five minutes with a sheaf of papers in his hand. "I believe we're ready to talk business, Mrs. Duncan. Mr. Duncan doesn't have enough in his checking account to cover the loan, so how were you proposing to pay it?"

"I have a trust fund, Mr. VanRoden. I transferred it from New York to another bank here in Billings. First, is the outstanding debt on the mortgage less than two hundred thousand?"

He coughed. "Yes, it is."

"Then I'll be back. I'm going to my bank now to have the trust fund transferred into my checking account. I've had full access to it since I was twenty-five, so there's no problem."

He pushed the telephone toward her. "Call them, so they'll let you in. They'll be closing for lunch shortly."

She smiled at him as she reached for the phone. "By the way, do you know a good obstetrician?"

A phone call later, it had been arranged for her to enter the other bank by a side door. An hour later she was back at the first bank, cashier's check in hand for the amount VanRoden had given her before she left.

She signed the necessary papers and walked out of the bank with the deed to the ranch and the papers that said the debt had been paid in full. She also had an appointment the following week with the obstetrician VanRoden's wife had used. She grinned as she got into the car. Contacts had their uses, even unlikely ones. Poor Mr. VanRoden had looked startled at being asked to recommend an obstetrician, then had offered his congratulations.

She had no illusions that everything was going to be fine now just because she had paid the mortgage. She hadn't done it lightly; she had done it with the full knowledge that Reese would be furious, but she was willing to fight for their future, their child's future. She had to deal with the scars left by Reese's first marriage, and this was far more serious than painting the house. As a matter of fact, he *had* drawn up a note stating that he would repay her for the cost of the paint and estimated labor, which she thought was ridiculous, but was a fair measure of how determined he was in the matter.

But knowing she had to tell him and knowing how to tell him were two different things. She couldn't just say, "I went into Billings today to make an appointment with an obstetrician because I'm pregnant, and by the way, while I was there I paid off the mortgage." On the other hand, that was certainly a good example of killing two birds with one stone.

She was still worrying it over in her mind when she got home at about four-thirty. There was no sign of Reese's truck, so perhaps she had made it without him even knowing she'd been gone. If he had come back to the house for any reason during the day, he'd ask questions as soon as he got back, and one thing she wouldn't do was lie to him. Delaying telling him about the mortgage was different from lying to him about it.

It was amazing how tired she was, and equally amazing how she could feel so exhausted but still feel well.

She would be having his baby sometime late in October or early in November, if she had figured correctly. The knowledge of it was like a great inner warmth, and she had never wanted anything more than to share it with him. Only the worry he had been enduring over the ranch had kept her from telling him, because she didn't want to give him something else to worry about. The stern lines in his face were deeper, and his eyes were habitually grim these days, as he faced losing everything he had worked so hard for, for so long. How could she burden him with the knowledge that now they had medical bills to consider, as well?

How could she *not* tell him?

As she changed clothes, her fatigue suddenly became overwhelming. She fought it, knowing that it was time to begin cooking dinner, but the thought of all that preparation made the fatigue even worse, and her stomach suddenly rolled. She broke out in a sweat and sank weakly onto the bed. What a great time for morning sickness to hit—late in the afternoon on a day when she needed all her wits about her. She sat there for a minute, and the nausea faded, but the fatigue was worse. There was no way she could summon the energy even to go downstairs; exhaustion pulled on her limbs and eyelids, dragging both down. With a sigh she stretched out on the bed, her eyes already closing. Just a short nap; that was all she needed.

Reese found her there. He had noticed that the kitchen light wasn't on when he got home, but he had taken care of the evening chores before going into the house. The kitchen was empty, with no sign of meal preparations in progress, and the house was strangely silent. "Maddie?" When there was no answer, a worried frown creased his forehead, and he searched the downstairs, then started up the stairs. "Maddie?"

He turned on the light in the bedroom, and there she was, curled on her side on the bed. She didn't stir even when the light came on. He'd never known her to nap during the day, and he was instantly alarmed. Was she sick? She had seemed okay that morning. He was dirty from the day's work, but he didn't care about that as he sat down on the side of the bed and turned her onto her back. She felt warm under his hands, but not unusually so. He shook her, and worry sharpened his tone. "Maddie, wake up!"

Slowly her lids drifted upward, and she sighed. "Reese," she murmured, but she couldn't keep her eyes open.

He shook her again. "Are you all right? Wake up."

Reluctantly she roused, lifting one hand to rub her eyes. "What time is it?" Then she looked at him again as realization sank in and said, "Oh my God, dinner!"

"Dinner can wait. Are you all right?"

Her heart lurched as she stared up at him. His face was lined and grayish with fatigue, but there was worry in his eyes, not irritation. Automatically she reached up to touch his cheek, stroking her fingers over the high ridge of his cheekbone. She loved everything about this man, even his stubborn temper. She took his hand and placed it on her belly. "I'm pregnant," she whispered. "We're having a baby."

His pupils dilated, and he looked down at his hand on her slender body. From the time she had stopped taking the birth control pills, every time he had made love to her he had been aware that he might impregnate her, but the reality of having her say she was pregnant was still almost a physical shock. His baby was growing under his hand, utterly protected in her flat little belly.

He slid off the bed onto his knees beside it, still dazed. "When?" he asked in a strained tone.

"The last week in October, or the first week in November."

He unsnapped her jeans and slid the zipper down, then spread the fly open so he could touch her skin. He pushed her sweatshirt up out of the way and slowly leaned forward, first pressing a light kiss to her belly, then resting his cheek against it. Madelyn stroked his hair and wondered if the baby would have dark coloring like him or her fairness. It was such a new, wonderful consideration, their child, created from the raw passion that still burned between them. Seven more months suddenly seemed too long to wait to hold it, to see Reese's powerful hands turn gentle as he cradled his child. "Do you want a boy or a girl?" she asked, still whispering, as if normal speech might spoil the sweetness of this moment.

"Does it matter?" He rubbed his rough cheek against her belly, his eyes closing as he luxuriated in the caress.

"Not to me."

"Or to me." Silence grew in the room as he fully absorbed the news; then finally he lifted his head. "Are you feeling sick?"

"I was a little nauseated, but mostly I was incredibly tired. I tried, but I just couldn't keep my eyes open," she said apologetically.

"Are you all right now?"

She thought about it, mentally taking stock of herself, then nodded. "All systems are go."

He moved back and let her get to her feet, then caught her to him and tilted her mouth up. The expression in his eyes was intense as he gave her a hard, brief kiss. "Are you certain?"

"I'm certain." She smiled and looped her arms around his neck, letting her weight swing from them.

"You'll know if I'm feeling sick. I'll turn green and keel over."

He cupped her bottom and held her against him as he kissed her again, and this time there was nothing brief about it. Madelyn held him tightly, her eyes closing as his familiar nearness sent warmth through her. She loved him so much it sometimes frightened her; she hoped he would remember that.

His lovemaking that night was achingly tender and incredibly prolonged. He couldn't seem to get enough of her, taking her again and again, staying inside her for a long time afterward. They finally went to sleep like that, with her leg thrown over his hip, and she thought it had never been more perfect than it was then, with Reese in her arms and his child in her womb.

A week later Reese walked back to the house from the barn with a defeated expression on his face. Madelyn watched him from the kitchen window and knew she couldn't put it off any longer. She simply couldn't let him worry any longer; better to enrage him than watch the lines settle deeper in his face every day. He would sit in his office for hours every night, going over and over the books, pacing and running his hands through his hair, then trying it again, only to come up with the same figures and no hope.

She heard him come in and take off his muddy boots; then he came into the kitchen in his sock feet. "The truck needs a new oil pump," he said tiredly.

She twisted the hand towel she was holding. "Then buy one." Tension was tightening her muscles, and she swallowed the faint rise of nausea.

His mouth was bitter. "Why bother? We won't be here another month anyway."

Slowly she hung up the towel then turned to face him, leaning back against the cabinet for support. "Yes, we will."

He thought he knew what she meant. He could call Robert—but Robert would have to be a fool to invest in the ranch now. He had put it off as long as he could, and now he didn't see anything else he could do. Madelyn was pregnant; she had her first doctor's appointment the next day, and money would be required up front. Then they were facing bills from the hospital, and he didn't have medical insurance. That had been one of the first things to go.

"I'll call Robert," he said gently. "But don't hope too much."

She put her shoulders back and took a deep breath. "Call Robert if you want, after I tell you what I have to tell you. You'll be in a different situation then and—" She stopped, looking at him helplessly, and began again. "I paid off the mortgage with my trust fund."

For a moment he didn't react at all, just watched her silently, and she started to hope. Then his eyes began to chill, and she braced herself.

"What?" he asked very softly.

"I paid off the mortgage. The papers are in my underwear drawer."

Without a word he turned and went upstairs. Madelyn followed, her heart pounding. She had faced his anger before without turning a hair, but this was different. This was striking at the very basis of his feelings.

He jerked her underwear drawer open just as she entered the bedroom. She hadn't stuffed the papers in the bottom; they were lying right there in plain sight. He picked them up and flipped through them, noting the amount and date on the documents.

He didn't look up. "How did you arrange it?"

"I went to Billings last week, the day you told me about the mortgage. Banks don't care who pays off loans so long as they get their money, and since I'm your wife they didn't question it."

"Did you think presenting me with a fait accompli would change my mind?"

She wished that he would stop using that soft voice. When Reese was angry he roared, and she could handle that, but this was something new.

His head came up, and she flinched. His eyes were like green ice. "Answer me."

She stood very still. "No, I didn't think anything would change your mind, and that's why I did it behind your back."

"You were right. Nothing would change my mind. I'll see you in hell before you get any part of this ranch."

"I don't want to take the ranch away from you. I've never wanted that."

"You've played your part well, Maddie, I'll give you that. You haven't complained, you've acted like a perfect wife. You even carried it so far as to pretend you love me."

"I do love you." She took a step toward him, her hands outstretched. "Listen—"

Suddenly the rage in him erupted, and he threw the sheaf of papers at her. They separated and swirled around her, then drifted to the floor. "That's what I think of your so-called 'love,'" he said with gritted teeth. "If you think doing something you knew I couldn't bear is an expression of 'love,' then you don't have any idea what the real thing is."

"I didn't want you to lose the ranch—"

"So you just took care of the mortgage. Any divorce court now would consider you a co-owner, wouldn't they? They'd figure I talked you into investing your inheritance and the prenuptial agreement wouldn't mean a damn. Hell, why should you get less than April? This isn't the operation it once was, but the land is worth a hell of a lot."

"I don't want a divorce, I haven't even thought of divorce," she said desperately. "I wanted to keep the ranch for you. At least this way you have a chance to rebuild it, if you'll just take it!"

He said sarcastically, "Yeah, if it's worth more, you'll get more."

"For the last time, I don't want a divorce!"

He reached out and pinched her chin, the gesture savagely playful. "You just might get one anyway, dollface, because I sure as hell don't want a wife who'd knife me in the back like that. You weren't my first choice, and I should have listened to my instincts, but you had me as hot as a sixteen-year-old after my first piece in the back seat. April was a bitch, but you're worse, Maddie, because you played along and pretended this was just what you wanted. Then you slipped the blade between my ribs so slick I never even saw it coming."

"This *is* what I want." She was pale, her eyes darkening.

"Well, you're not what I want. You're hot between the sheets, but you don't have what it takes to be a ranch wife," he said cruelly.

"Reese Duncan, if you're trying to run me off, you're doing a good job of it," she warned shakily.

He raised his eyebrows. His tone was icily polite. "Where would you like to go? I'll give you a ride."

"If you'll climb down off that mountain of pride you'll see how wrong you are! I don't want to take the ranch away. I want to live here and raise our children here. You and I aren't the only ones involved in this. I'm carrying your baby, and it's his heritage, too!"

His eyes went black as he remembered the baby, and his gaze swept down her slender figure. "On second thought, you aren't going anywhere. You're staying right here until that baby's born. Then I don't care what the hell *you* do, but my kid is staying with me."

Coldness settled inside her, pushing away the hurt and anger that had been building with every word he said. Understanding could go only so far. Sympathy held out only so long. He didn't love her, and he didn't believe in her love for him, so exactly how much of a marriage did they have? One made of mirrors and moonshine, and held together by sex. She stared at him, her eyes going blank. Later there would be pain, but not now.

She said very carefully, "When you calm down you'll regret saying this."

"The only thing I regret is marrying you." He took her purse from the top of the dresser and opened it.

"What are you looking for?" She made no effort to grab it from him. In any test of strength against him she would be humiliated.

He held up the car keys. "These." He dropped her purse and shoved the keys into his pocket. "Like I said, you're not going anywhere with my kid inside you. The only moving you're doing is out of my bed. There are three other bedrooms. Pick one, and keep your butt in it."

He stalked from the room, being very careful not to touch her. Madelyn sank down on the bed, her legs folding under her like spaghetti. She could barely breathe, and dark spots swam in front of her eyes. Cold chills made her shake.

She didn't know how long it was before her mind began to function again, but finally it did, slowly at first, then with gathering speed. She began to get angry, a calm, deep, slow-burning anger that grew until it had destroyed all the numbness.

She got up and began methodically moving her things out of Reese's bedroom and into the room where she had slept the night she had visited him. She didn't move a few token things in the hope that he would get over his temper, reconsider and tell her to stay put; she purged the bedroom of all signs of her presence. She left the mortgage papers lying where they were in the middle of the room. Let him walk over them if he didn't want to pick them up.

If he wanted war, she'd give him war.

Pride prompted her to stay in her bedroom and not speak to him; pregnancy insisted that she eat. She went downstairs and cooked a full meal in an effort to rub a little salt in his wounds. If he didn't want to eat what she had prepared, then he could either do it himself or do without.

But he came to the table when she called him and ate his usual hearty meal. As she was clearing the dishes away she said, "Don't forget the doctor's appointment in the morning."

He didn't look at her. "I'll drive you. You aren't getting the keys back."

"Fine."

Then she went upstairs, showered and went to bed.

The next morning they didn't speak a word all the way to Billings. When her name was called in the doctor's office, which was filled with women in various stages of pregnancy, she got up and walked past him to follow the nurse. He turned his head, watching the graceful sway of her retreating figure. In a few months she would lose her grace and the sway would become a waddle. His hand tightened into a fist, and it was all he could do to keep from swearing aloud. *How could she have done that to him?*

Madelyn was questioned, stuck, checked, probed and measured. When she had dressed she was directed into the doctor's office, and in a moment Reese joined her, followed shortly by the doctor.

"Well, everything looks normal," the doctor said, consulting his charts. "You're in good physical shape, Mrs. Duncan. Your uterus is enlarged more like thirteen or fourteen weeks than the nine or ten you think it should be, so you may be off on your conception date. We'll do an ultrasound when you're further along to get a better idea of the baby's maturity. It could just be a large baby, or twins. I see that your maternal grandmother was a twin, and multiple births usually follow the female line."

Reese sat up straight, his eyes sharpening. "Is there any danger in having twins?"

"Not much. They usually come a little early, and we have to be careful about that. At this stage of the game, I'm more worried about a large baby than I am twins. Your wife should be able to have twins without a problem, as their birth weight is usually lower than that of a single baby. The total is more, but the individual weights are less. How much did you weigh when you were born, Mr. Duncan?"

"Ten pounds, two ounces." His mouth was grim.

"I'll want to keep a very close eye on your wife if this baby approaches a birth weight of anything over eight pounds. She has a narrow pelvis, not drastically so, but a ten-pound baby would probably require a C-section."

That said, he began talking to Madelyn about her diet, vitamins and rest, and he gave her several booklets about prenatal care. When they left half an hour later, Madelyn was weighted down with prescriptions and reading material. Reese drove to a pharmacy, where he had the prescriptions filled, then headed home again. Madelyn sat straight and silent beside him. When they got home, he realized that she hadn't looked at him once all day.

11

The next morning as he started to leave she asked coolly, "Can you hear the car horn blow from anywhere on the ranch?"

He looked startled. "Of course not." He eyed her questioningly, but she still wasn't looking at him.

"Then how am I supposed to find you or contact you?"

"Why would you want to?" he asked sarcastically.

"I'm pregnant. I could fall, or start to miscarry. Any number of things."

It was an argument he couldn't refute. He set his jaw, faced with the choice between giving her the means to leave or endangering both her life and that of his baby. When it came down to it, he didn't have a choice. He took the keys from his pocket and slammed them down on the cabinet, but he kept his hand on them.

"Do I have your word you won't run?"

She looked at him finally, but her eyes were cool and blank. "No. Why should I waste my breath making promises when you wouldn't believe me anyway?"

"Just what is it you want me to believe? That you haven't worked it so you have just as much claim to the ranch as I have? A woman made a fool of me once and walked away with half of everything I owned, but it won't happen again, even if I have to burn this house to the ground and sell the land for a loss, is that clear?'' He was shouting by the time he finished, and he looked at her as if he hated the sight of her.

Madelyn didn't show any expression or move. "If that was all I'd wanted, I could have paid off the mortgage at any time.''

Her point scored; she saw it in his eyes. She could have followed it up, but she held her peace. She had given him something to think about. She would give him a lot more to think about before this was over.

He banged out of the house, leaving the car keys on the cabinet. She picked them up, tossing them in her hand as she went upstairs to the bedroom, where she already had some clothes packed. In the two nights she had spent alone in this room, she had thought through what she was going to do and where she was going to go. Reese would expect her to go running back to New York now that she had a claim on the ranch, but she had never even considered that. To teach him the lesson he needed, she had to be close by.

It would be just like him to deliberately work close by in case she tried to leave, so she didn't, and felt fierce satisfaction when he came home for lunch after telling her that he would be out all day. Since she hadn't cooked anything, she made a plate of sandwiches and put it in front of him, then continued with what she had been doing before, which was cleaning the oven.

He asked, "Aren't you going to eat?''

"I've already eaten.''

A few minutes later he asked, "Should you be doing work like that?''

"It isn't hard."

Her cool tone discouraged any more conversational overtures. She wasn't letting him off that easy. She had told him twice that she wasn't going to pay for April's sins, but it evidently hadn't sunk in; now she was going to show him.

When he left again she waited half an hour, then carried her suitcase out to the car. She didn't have far to go, and it wouldn't take him long to find her, a few days at the most. Then he could take the car back if he wanted, so she didn't feel guilty about it. Besides, she didn't need it. She fully expected to be back at the ranch before her next doctor's appointment, but if she wasn't, then she would inform Reese that he had to take her. Her plan had nothing to do with staying away from him.

There was a room above Floris's café that was always for rent, because there was never anyone in Crook who needed to rent it. It would do for her for as long as she needed it. She drove to Crook and parked the car in front of the café. The idea wasn't to hide from Reese; she wanted him to know exactly where she was.

She went into the café, but there wasn't anyone behind the counter. "Floris? Is anyone here?"

"Hold your water," came Floris's unmistakable sour voice from the kitchen. A few minutes later she came through the door. "You want coffee, or something to eat?"

"I want to rent the room upstairs."

Floris stopped and narrowed her eyes at Madelyn. "What do you want to do that for?"

"Because I need a place to stay."

"You've got a big house back on that ranch, and a big man to keep you warm at night, if that's all you need."

"What I have," Madelyn said very clearly, "is a pigheaded husband who needs to be taught a lesson."

"Hmmph. Never seen a man yet wasn't pigheaded."

"I'm pregnant, too."

"Does he know?"

"He does."

"He knows where you are?"

"He will soon. I'm not hiding from him. He'll probably come through the door breathing fire and raising hell, but I'm not going back until he understands a few things."

"Such as?"

"Such as I'm not his first wife. He got a dirty deal, but I'm not the one who gave it to him, and I'm tired of paying for someone else's dirt."

Floris looked her up and down, then nodded, and a pleased expression for once lit her sour face. "All right, the room's yours. I always did like to see a man get his comeuppance," she muttered as she turned to go back into the kitchen. Then she stopped and looked back at Madelyn. "You got any experience as a short-order cook?"

"No. Do you need one?"

"Wouldn't have asked if I didn't. I'm doing the cooking and waitressing, too. That sorry Lundy got mad because I told him his eggs were like rubber and quit on me last week."

Madelyn considered the situation and found she liked it. "I could wait on tables."

"You ever done that before?"

"No, but I've taken care of Reese for nine months."

Floris grunted. "I guess that qualifies you. He don't strike me as an easy man to satisfy. Well, you in good health? I don't want you on your feet if you're having trouble keeping that baby."

"Perfect health. I saw a doctor yesterday."

"Then the job's yours. I'll show you the room. It's nothing fancy, but it's warm during the winter."

The room was clean and snug, and that was about the limit of its virtues, but Madelyn didn't mind. There was a single bed, a couch, a card table with two chairs, a hot plate and a minuscule bathroom with cracking tile. Floris turned on the heat so it would get warm and returned to the kitchen while Madelyn carried her suitcases in. After hanging up her clothes in the small closet, she went downstairs to the café, tied an apron around her and took up her duties as waitress.

When Reese got home that night he was dead tired; he'd been kicked, stepped on and had a rope burn on his arm. The cows would begin dropping their spring calves any time, and that would be even more work, especially if a cold front moved in.

When he saw that the car was gone and the house was dark, it was like taking a kick in the chest, punching the air out of him. He stared at the dark windows, filled with a paralyzing mixture of pain and rage. He hadn't really thought she would leave. Deep down, he had expected her to stay and fight it out, toe-to-toe and chin to chin, the way she'd done so many times. Instead she'd left, and he closed his eyes at the piercing realization that she was exactly what he'd most feared: a grasping, shallow woman who wasn't able to take the hard times. She'd run back to the city and her cushy life-style, the stylish clothes.

And she'd taken his baby with her.

It was a betrayal ten times worse than anything April had done to him. He had begun to trust Maddie, begun to let himself think of their future in terms of years rather than just an unknown number of months. She had lain beneath him and willingly let him get her pregnant; for most of a year she had lived with him, cooked for him, washed his clothes, laughed and teased and worked alongside him, slept in his arms.

Then she had stabbed him in the back. It was a living nightmare, and he was living it for the second time.

He walked slowly into the house, his steps dragging. There were no warm, welcoming smells in the kitchen, no sound except for the hum of the refrigerator and the ticking of the clock. Despite everything, he had a desperate, useless hope that she'd had to go somewhere, that there was a note of explanation somewhere in the house. He searched all the rooms, but there was no note. He went into the bedroom where she had spent the past two nights and found the dresser drawers empty, the bathroom swept clean of the fragrant female paraphernalia. He was still trying to get used to not seeing her clothes in the closet beside his; to find them nowhere in the house was staggering.

It was like pouring salt into an open wound, but he went into the other bedroom where she had stored her "New York" clothes. It was as if he had to check every missing sign of her inhabitance to verify her absence,

a wounded and bewildered animal sniffing around for
his mate before he sat down and howled his anger and
loss at the world.

But when he opened the closet door he stared at the
row of silk blouses, hung on satin-padded hangers and
protected by plastic covers, the chic suits and loung-
ing pajamas, the high-heeled shoes in a dozen colors
and styles. A faint hint of her perfume wafted from
the clothes, and he broke out in a sweat, staring at
them.

Swiftly he went downstairs. Her books were still
here, and her stereo system. She might be gone now,
but she had left a lot of her things here, and that
meant she would be back. She would probably come
back during the day, when she would expect him to be
gone, so she could pack the rest and leave without ever
seeing him.

But if she were going back to New York, as she almost certainly had been planning, why had she taken
her ranch clothes and left the city clothes?

Who knew why Madelyn did anything? he thought
wearily. Why had she paid off the mortgage with her
trust fund when she knew that was the one thing, given
his past, that he would be unable to bear?

He'd never in his life been angrier, not even when he
had sat in a courtroom and heard a judge hand over
half his ranch to April. He hadn't expected anything
better from April, who had given him ample demon-
stration of just how vindictive and callous she could
be. But when Maddie had blindsided him like that, she
had really hit him hard and low, and he was still reel-
ing. Every time he tried to think about it, the pain and

anger were so great that they crowded out everything else.

Well, she was gone, so he'd have plenty of time to think about it now. But she would have a hell of a time getting back in to get her things while he was gone, because the first chance he got he was going to change the locks on the house.

For now, however, he was going to do something he hadn't done even when April had done such a good job of wrecking his life. He was going to get the bottle of whiskey that had been in the cupboard for so many years and get dead drunk. Maybe then he would be able to sleep without Maddie beside him.

He felt like hell the next day, with a pounding head and a heaving stomach, but he dragged himself up and took care of the animals; it wasn't their fault he was a damn fool. By the time his headache began to fade and he began to feel halfway human again, it was too late to go to the general store to buy new locks.

The next day the cows began dropping their calves. It was the same every time: when the first one went into labor and drifted away to find a quiet place to calve, the others one by one followed suit. And they could pick some of the damnedest places to have their calves. It was an almost impossible task for one man to track down the cows in their hiding places, make certain the little newborns were all right, help the cows who were in difficulty and take care of the calves who were born dead or sickly. Instinct always went wrong with at least one cow, and she would refuse to have anything to do with her new baby, meaning Reese had to either get another cow to adopt it or take it to the barn for hand-feeding.

It was three days before he had a minute to rest, and when he did he dropped down on the couch in an exhausted stupor and slept for sixteen hours.

It was almost a week after Madelyn had left before he finally got time to drive to Crook. The pain and anger had become an empty, numb feeling in his chest.

The first thing he saw as he passed Floris's café was the white Ford station wagon parked out front.

His heart lurched wildly, and the bottom dropped out of his stomach. She was back, probably on her way to get the rest of her things. He parked next door in front of the general store and stared at the car, his fingers drumming on the steering wheel. The familiar anger exploded into the numb vacuum, and something became immediately, blindingly clear to him.

He wasn't going to let her go. If he had to fight her in every court in the country, he was going to keep his ranch intact and she was going to stay his wife. He'd been glad to see the last of April, but there was no way he was going to let Maddie just walk out. She was carrying his baby, a baby that was going to grow up in his house if he had to tie Maddie to the bed every day when he left.

He got out of the truck and strode toward the café, his boot heels thudding on the wooden sidewalk, his face set.

He pushed open the door and walked inside, standing in the middle of the room as he surveyed the booths and tables. There was no long-legged blonde with a lazy smile at any of them, though two lean and bandy-legged cowboys straddled stools at the counter.

Then the kitchen door opened and his long-legged blonde came through it, wrapped in an apron and carrying two plates covered with enormous hamburgers and mounds of steaming French fries. She flicked a glance at him and neither changed expression or missed a beat as she set the plates in front of the cowboys. "Here you go. Let me know if you want any pie. Floris baked an apple cobbler this morning that'll make you cry, it tastes so good."

Then she looked at him with those blank, cool eyes and said, "What can I get for you?"

The cowboys looked around, and one coughed when he saw who Madelyn was talking to; Reese pretty well knew everybody in a hundred-mile range, and they knew him, too, by sight if not personally. Everyone also knew Madelyn; a woman with her looks and style didn't go unnoticed, so it was damn certain those two cowboys realized it was her husband standing behind them looking like a thunderstorm about to spit lightning and hail all over them.

In a calm, deadly voice Reese said, "Bring me a cup of coffee," and went over to fold his long length into one of the booths.

She brought it immediately, sliding the coffee and a glass of water in front of him. Then she gave him an impersonal smile that didn't reach her eyes and said, "Anything else?" She was already turning to go as she said it.

He snapped his hand out, catching her wrist and pulling her to a halt. He felt the slenderness of her bones under his fingers and was suddenly, shockingly aware of how physically overmatched she was with him, yet she had never backed away from him. Even in bed, when he had held her slim hips in his hands and thrust heavily into her, she had wrapped those legs around him and taken everything he could give her. Maddie wasn't the type to run, unless leaving was something she had planned from the beginning. But if that were so, why was she here? Why hadn't she gone back to New York, out of his reach?

"Sit down," he said in a low, dangerous voice.

"I have work to do."

"I said to sit down." Using his grip on her wrist, he pulled her down into the booth. She was still watching him with those cool, distant eyes.

"What are you doing here?" he snapped, ignoring the looks the two cowboys were giving him.

"I work here."

"That's what I meant. What the *hell* are you doing working here?"

"Supporting myself. What did you expect me to do?"

"I expected you to keep your little butt on the ranch like I told you to."

"Why should I stay where I'm not wanted? By the way, if you can figure out a way to get the car home, feel free to take it. I don't need it."

With an effort he controlled the anger and impatience building in him. It might be just what she wanted, for him to lose his temper in a public place.

"Where are you staying?" he asked in a voice that showed the strain he was under.

"Upstairs."

"Get your clothes. You're going home with me."

"No."

"What did you say?"

"I said no. N-O. It's a two-letter word signifying refusal."

He flattened his hands on the table to keep himself from grabbing her and giving her a good shaking, or from pulling her onto his lap and kissing her senseless. Right at the moment, he wasn't certain which it would be. "I'm not putting up with this, Maddie. Get upstairs and get your clothes." Despite himself, he couldn't keep his voice down, and the two cowboys were openly staring at him.

She slid out of the booth and was on her feet before he could grab her, and he was reminded that, when she chose, Maddie could move like the wind. "Give me one good reason why I should!" she fired back at him, the chill in her eyes beginning to heat now.

"Because you're carrying my baby!" he roared, surging to his own feet.

"You're the one who said, quote, that you didn't care what the hell I did and that you regret marrying me, unquote. I was carrying the baby then, too, so what's different now?"

"I changed my mind."

"Well, bully for you! You also told me that I'm not what you want and I don't have what it takes to be a ranch wife. That's another quote."

One of the cowboys cleared his throat. "You sure look like you've got what it takes to me, Miss Maddie."

Reese rounded on the cowboy with death in his eyes and his fist clenched. "Do you want to wear your teeth or carry them?" he asked in an almost soundless voice.

The cowboy still seemed to be having trouble with his throat. He cleared it again, but it took him two tries before he managed to say, "Just making a comment."

"Then make it outside. This is between me and my wife."

In the West, a man broke his own horses and killed his own snakes, and everybody else kept their nose the hell out of his business. The cowboy fumbled in his pocket for a couple of bills and laid them on the counter. "Let's go," he said to his friend.

"You go on." The other cowboy forked up a fry covered in ketchup. "I'm not through eating." *Or watching the show, either.*

Floris came through the kitchen door, her sour expression intact and a spatula in her hand. "Who's making all the noise out here?" she demanded; then her gaze fell on Reese. "Oh, it's you." She made it sound as if he were about as welcome as the plague.

"I've come to take Maddie home," he said.

"Don't see why she'd want to go, you being so sweet-tempered and all."

"She's my wife."

"She can wait on men here and get paid for it." She shook the spatula at him. "What have you got to offer her besides that log in your pants?"

Reese's jaw was like granite. He could toss Madelyn over his shoulder and carry her home, but even though he was willing to bully her, he didn't want to physically force her. For one thing, she was pregnant, but more importantly, he wanted her to go home with him because she wanted to. One look at her face told him that she wasn't going to willingly take a step toward the ranch.

Well, he knew where she was now. She hadn't gone back to New York. She was within reach, and he wasn't giving up. With one last violent look at her, he threw his money on the table and stomped out.

Madelyn slowly let out the breath she'd been holding. That had been close. He was evidently as determined to take her back to the ranch as he was to believe she was a clone of his first wife. And if she knew one thing about Reese Duncan, it was that he was as stubborn as any mule, and he didn't give up. He'd be back.

She picked up his untouched coffee and carried it back to the counter. Floris looked at the door that was still quivering from the force with which Reese had slammed it, then turned to Madelyn with the most incredible expression on her face. It was like watching the desert floor crack as her leathered skin moved and rearranged itself, and a look of unholy glee came into her eyes. The two cowboys watched in shock as Floris actually smiled.

The older woman held out her hand, palm up and fingers stiffly extended. Madelyn slapped her own hand down on it in victory, then reversed the position for Floris's slap as they gave each other a congratulatory low five.

"Wife one, husband zero," Floris said with immense satisfaction.

He was back the next day, sliding into a booth and watching her with hooded eyes as she took care of the customers. The little café was unusually busy today, and he wondered with a sourness that would have done credit to Floris if it was because word of their confrontation the day before had spread. There was nothing like a free floor show to draw people in.

She looked tired today, and he wondered if she'd been sick. She'd had a few bouts of nausea before she'd left, but her morning sickness hadn't been full-blown. From the way she looked now, it was getting there. It made him even angrier, because if she'd been at home where she belonged she would have been able to lie down and rest.

Without asking, she brought a cup of coffee to him and turned to go. Like a replay of the day before, his hand shot out and caught her. He could almost feel everyone's attention fastening on them like magnets. "Have you been sick?" he asked roughly.

"This morning. It passed when Floris fed me some dry toast. Excuse me, I have other customers."

He let her go because he didn't want another scene like yesterday's. He sipped the coffee and watched her as she moved among the customers, dispensing a smile here and a teasing word there, drawing laughter and making faces light up. That was a talent of hers, find-ing amusement in little things and inviting others to share it with her, almost enticing them. She had done the same thing to him, he realized. The nine months she'd spent with him had been the most contented of his life, emotionally and physically.

He wanted her back. He wanted to watch the lazy way she strolled around the house and accomplished miracles without seeming to put forth much effort at all. He wanted her teasing him, waking him up with some outlandish bit of trivia and expecting him to match it. He wanted to pull her beneath him, spread her legs and penetrate her body with his, make her

admit that she still loved him and would rather be with
him than anywhere else.

He didn't understand why she wasn't in New York,
why she had only come as far as Crook and stopped,
knowing he would soon find her. Hell, running to
Crook wasn't running away at all, it was simply moving a little piece down the road.

The only answer was that she had never intended to
go back to New York. She hadn't wanted the big city;
she had just wanted to get away from him.

The memory of all he'd said to her played in his
mind, and he almost flinched. She remembered every
word of it, too; she had even quoted some of them
back to him. She'd told him at the time that he would
regret saying them, but he'd been too enraged, feeling
too betrayed, to pay any attention to her. He should
have remembered that Maddie gave as good as she got.

She could so easily have gone to New York; she had
the money in her checking account to do whatever she
wanted, and Robert would welcome her back without
question. So if she had stayed it had to be because she
liked living in Montana. Even the question of revenge
could just as easily have been played out from New
York as from Crook, because it was her absence from
his house that was punishing him. The emptiness of it
was driving him crazy.

Eventually she came back by with the coffeepot to
refill his cup and ask, "Do you want some pie with
that? It's fresh coconut today."

"Sure." It would give him an excuse to stay longer.

The café eventually had to clear out some. The customers had other things they had to do, and Reese
hadn't done anything interesting enough to make them

stay. When Madelyn coasted by to pick up his empty dessert saucer and refill his cup she asked, "Don't you have any work to do?"

"Plenty. The cows dropped their spring calves."

Just for a second her eyes lit; then she shrugged and turned away. He said, "Wait. Sit down a minute and rest. You haven't been off your feet since I got here and that's been—" he stopped to check his watch "—two hours ago."

"It's been busy this morning. You don't stop working a herd just because you want to rest, do you?"

Despite himself, he couldn't help grinning at her comparison between a herd of cattle and her customers. "Sit down anyway. I'm not going to yell at you."

"Well, that's a change," she muttered, but she sat down across from him and propped her feet on the seat beside him, stretching her legs out. He lifted her feet and placed them on his knee, rubbing the calves of her legs under the table and holding her firmly in place when she automatically tried to pull away.

"Just relax," he said quietly. "Should you be on your feet this much?"

"I'd be on my feet if I were still at the ranch. I didn't cook sitting down, you know. I feel fine. I'm just pregnant, not incapacitated." But she closed her eyes as his kneading fingers worked at her tired muscles; he had a good touch, one learned from years of working with animals.

He had a good touch in bed, too. Every woman should have a lover like Reese, wild and hungry, as generous with his own body as he was demanding of hers. The memories pooled in her stomach like lava, raising her temperature, and her eyes popped open. If she let herself think about it too much, she would be in his lap before she knew what she was doing.

Reese said, "I want you to come home with me."

If he had been angrily demanding she could have met him with her own anger, but his quiet tone invited instead of demanded. She sighed and leaned her elbows on the table. "My answer is still the same. Give me one good reason why I should."

"And my answer is still the same. You're carrying my baby. It deserves to have its heritage, to grow up on the ranch. You even told me that was one of the reasons you paid the mortgage, to preserve the ranch for our children."

"I haven't taken the baby away from Montana," she pointed out. "I haven't even gone far from the ranch. The baby will have you and the ranch, but I don't have to live there for that to be possible."

"Miss Maddie, you got any more of that coffee?" a customer called, and she pulled her feet down from his lap without another word, going about her business with a smile.

Reese finally gave up and went home, but he tossed in the big bed all night, thinking of her breasts and the way she tasted, the way it felt to slide into her and feel her tight inner clinging, hear the soft sounds she made as he brought her to pleasure.

He had to mend fences the next day, and he worked automatically, his mind still on Maddie, trying to figure out how to get her back.

She'd made a telling point when she had asked him why she hadn't paid the mortgage before, if all she'd wanted had been a legal interest in the ranch that

would override any prenuptial agreement, and now he
had to ask himself the same thing. If that was all she'd
wanted, why had she waited nine months? Why had
she chased chickens and cows, fought blizzards and
risked her own life to save his if she'd been planning
on getting out? Even more telling, why had she gone
off her birth control pills and let him get her pregnant? That baby she carried was a planned baby, one
they had talked about and agreed to have. A woman
didn't deliberately get pregnant if she'd been planning to spend only a few months and then get out. The
land was worth a fortune; if money had been all she
wanted, paying off the mortgage had entitled her to a
great deal without the added, admittedly powerful,
asset of a pregnancy. No, she had gotten pregnant only
because she'd wanted this baby, and she had paid off
the mortgage for one reason: to save the ranch for
him, Reese Duncan. She might say she was saving her
child's heritage, but the baby was still an abstract, an
unknown person, however powerful her budding maternal instincts were. She had saved the ranch for her
husband, not her child.

Beyond that, Maddie didn't need money. With
Robert Cannon for a stepbrother, she could have anything she wanted just by asking. Robert Cannon had
money that made April's family look like two-bit pik-
ers.

It all kept coming back to the same thing, the same
question. Why had she paid the mortgage, knowing
how dead set he was against it, if she hadn't been
planning to file for divorce? The answer was always
the same, and she had given it to him. She had never
tried to hide it. She loved him.

The realization staggered him anew, and he had to stop to wipe the sweat from his face, even though the temperature was only in the thirties. Maddie loved him. She had tried to tell him when he'd been yelling all those insults at her, and he hadn't listened.

Savagely he jerked the wire tight and hammered in the staple to hold it. Crow had a bitter taste to it, but he was going to have to eat a lot of it if he wanted Maddie to come back to him. He'd gone off the deep end and acted as if she were just like April, even though he knew better. April had never enjoyed living in Montana, while Maddie had wallowed in it like a delighted child. This was the life she wanted.

She loved him enough to take the chance on paying off the mortgage, knowing how angry he would be but doing it anyway because it would save the ranch for him. She had put him before herself, and that was the true measure of love, but he'd been too much of a blind, stubborn ass to admit it.

His temper had gotten him into a hell of a mess, and he didn't have anyone to blame but himself. He had to stop letting April's greed blight his life; he had to stop seeing other people through April-embittered eyes. That was the worst thing she had done to him, not ruining him financially, but ruining the way he had seen other people. He'd even admitted it to himself the day he had met Maddie; if he had run across her before marrying April, he would have been after her with every means at his disposal, and he would have gotten her, too. He would have chased her across every state in the country if necessary, and put her in his bed before she could get away. As it was, he hadn't been able to resist her for long. Even if the schoolteacher—he couldn't even remember her name—had said yes, he would have found some way of getting out of it. Maddie had been the only one he'd wanted wearing his name from the minute he'd seen her.

Damn. If only foresight were as clear as hindsight, he could have saved himself a big helping of crow.

12

He walked into the café and immediately every eye turned toward him. He was beginning to feel like a damn outcast, the way everyone stopped talking and stared at him whenever he showed his face in town. Floris had come out of the kitchen and was arguing with one of the customers, who had ordered something she thought was stupid, from what he could hear, but she stopped yammering and stared at him, too. Then she abruptly turned and went back into the kitchen, probably to get her spatula.

Madelyn didn't acknowledge him, but no more than a minute had passed before a cup of hot coffee was steaming in front of him. She looked so good it was all he could do to keep from grabbing her. Her hair was in a loose French braid down her back, she wore those loose, chic, pleated jeans and a pair of deck shoes, and an oversize khaki shirt with the shirttails knotted at her waist, the collar turned up and the sleeves rolled, an outfit that looked impossibly stylish even under the apron she wore. He took a closer look at the shirt and scowled. It was *his* shirt! Damn it, when she'd left him she'd taken some of his clothes!

No doubt about it. He had to get that woman back, if only for the sake of his wardrobe.

A few minutes later she put a slice of chocolate pie on the table, and he picked up his fork with a hidden smile. They might be separated, but she was still trying to feed him. He'd always been a little startled by the way she had fussed over him and seen to his comfort, as if she had to protect him. Since he was a great deal bigger than she, it had always seemed incongruous to him. His own protective instincts worked overtime where she was concerned, too, so he supposed it evened out.

Finally he caught her eye and indicated the seat across from him with a jerk of his chin. Her eyebrows lifted at the arrogant summons, and she ignored him. He sighed. Well, what had he expected? He should have learned by now that Maddie didn't respond well to orders—unless she wanted to, for her own reasons.

There was evidently a rush hour in Crook now, at least judging by the number of customers who found it necessary to stop by the café. He wondered dourly if there was an alert system to signal everyone in the county when his truck was parked out front. It was over an hour before the place began to empty, but he waited patiently. The next time she came over with a refill of coffee he said, "Talk to me, Maddie. Please."

Perhaps it was the "please" that got to her, because she gave him a startled look and sat down. Floris came out of the kitchen and surveyed Reese with her hands on her hips, as if wondering why he was still there. He winked at her, the first time he'd ever done anything that playful, and her face filled with outrage just before she whirled to go back to the kitchen.

Maddie laughed softly, having seen the byplay. "You're in her bad books now, listed under 'Sorry Low-Down Husbands Who Play Around.'"

He grunted. "What was I listed under before, 'Sorry Low-Down Husbands Who Don't Play Around'?"

"'Yet,'" she added. "Floris doesn't have a high opinion of men."

"I've noticed." He looked her over closely, examining her face. "How do you feel today?"

"Fine. That's the first thing everyone asks me every day. Being pregnant is a fairly common occurrence, you know, but you'd think no other woman in this county had ever had a baby."

"No one's ever had *my* baby before, so I'm entitled to be interested." He reached across the table and took her hand, gently folding her fingers over his. She was still wearing her wedding ring. For that matter, he was still wearing his. It was the only jewelry he'd ever worn in his life, but he'd liked the looks of that thin gold band on his hand almost as much as he had liked the way his ring looked on Maddie. He played with the ring, twisting it on her finger, reminding her of its presence. "Come home with me, Maddie."

Same tune, same lyrics. She smiled sadly as she repeated her line. "Give me one good reason why I should."

"Because you love me." He said it gently, his fingers tightening on hers. That was the most powerful argument he could think of, the one she couldn't deny.

"I've always loved you. That isn't new. I loved you when I packed my clothes and walked out the door. If it wasn't reason enough to stay, why should it be reason enough to go back?"

Her gray, gray eyes were calm as she looked at him. His chest tightened as he realized it wasn't going to work. She wasn't going to come back to him no matter what argument he used. He'd been on a roller-coaster of hope since the day he had seen the station wagon parked out front, but suddenly he was plunging down a deep drop that didn't have an end. Dear God, had he ruined the best thing that had ever happened to him because he hadn't been able to accept it?

There was a thick knot in his throat; he had to swallow before he could speak again. "Do you...do you mind if I check up on you every day or so? Just to make sure you're feeling okay. And I'd like to go with you when you have a doctor's appointment, if you don't mind."

Now Maddie had to swallow at her sudden impulse to cry. She had never seen Reese diffident before, and she didn't like it. He was bold and arrogant and quick-tempered, and that was just the way she wanted him, as long as he realized a few important facts about their marriage. "This is your baby, too, Reese. I'd never try to cut you out."

He sighed, still playing with her fingers. "I was wrong, sweetheart. I have a phobia about the ranch after what April did to me—I know, you're not April, and I shouldn't take it out on you for what she did eight years ago. You told me, but I didn't listen. So tell me now what I can do to make it up to you."

"Oh, Reese, it isn't a matter of making anything up to me," she cried softly. "I don't have a scorecard with points on it, and after you tally up so many I'll move back to the ranch. It's about us, our relationship, and whether we have any future together."

"Then tell me what you're still worried about. Baby, I can't fix it if I don't know what it is."

"If you don't know what it is, then nothing *can* fix it."

"Are we down to riddles now? I'm not any good at mind reading," he warned. "Whatever you want, just say it right out. I can deal with reality, but guessing games aren't my strong suit."

"I'm not jerking you around. I'm not happy with this situation, either, but I'm not going back until I know for certain we have a future. That's the way it is, and I won't change my mind."

Slowly he stood up and pulled some bills out of his pocket. Maddie held up her hand dismissively. "Never mind, this one's on me. I get good tips," she said with a crooked smile.

He looked down at her with a surge of hunger that almost took him apart, and he didn't try to resist it. He leaned down and covered her mouth with his, tilting her head back so he could slant his lips more firmly over hers, his tongue sliding between her automatically parted lips. They had made love too often, their senses were too attuned to each other, for it to be anything but overwhelmingly right. She made one of her soft little sounds, and her tongue played with his, her mouth responding. If they had been alone the kiss would have ended in lovemaking; it was that simple, that powerful. No other woman in his life had ever gotten to him the way Maddie did.

The café was totally silent as the few customers still there watched with bated breath. The situation between Reese Duncan and his spirited wife was the best entertainment the county had seen in years.

"Harrummph!"

Reese lifted his head, his lips still shiny from the kiss. The loud interruption had come from Floris, who had left the sanctuary of the kitchen to protect her waitress. At least that was what Reese thought, since she had bypassed the spatula in favor of a butcher knife.

"I don't hold with none of that carrying-on in my place," she said, scowling at him.

He straightened and said softly but very clearly, "Floris, what you need is a good man to give you some loving and cure that sour disposition."

The smile she gave him was truly evil in intent. She gestured with the butcher knife. "The last fool that tried drew back a nub."

It always happened. Some people just didn't know when to keep out of something. The cowboy who had gotten in the argument with her the first time Reese had brought Maddie in just had to stick his oar in now. "Yeah, when was that, Floris?" he asked. "Before or after the Civil War?"

She turned on him like a she-bear on fresh meat. "Hell, boy, it was your daddy, and you're the best he could do with what he had left!"

It was the end of April. Spring was coming on fast, but Reese couldn't take the pleasure in the rebirth of the land that he usually did. He rattled around in the house, more acutely aware of its emptiness now than he had ever been before. He was busy, but he wasn't content. Maddie still wasn't home.

She had given him financial security with her legacy from her grandmother. Without the remaining payments of the huge mortgage hanging over him, he could use the money from the sale of last year's beef to expand, just as he had originally planned. For that matter, he could take out another loan with the ranch as collateral and start large-scale ranching again, with enough cowhands to help him do it right. Because of

Maddie, he could now put the ranch back on a par with what it used to be, even with the reduced acreage. She had never seen it as it had been, probably couldn't imagine the bustle and life in a large, profitable cattle ranch.

He needed to make some sort of decision and make it soon. If he were going to expand, he needed to get working on it right now.

But his heart wasn't in it. As much as he had always loved ranching, as deeply as his soul was planted in this majestically beautiful range, he didn't have the enthusiasm for it that he'd always had before. Without Maddie, he didn't much care.

But she was right; it was their baby's heritage. For that reason he had to take care of it to the best of his ability.

Life was always a fluid series of options. The circumstances and options might change from day to day, but there was always a set of choices to be made, and now he had to make a very important one.

If he expanded on his own it would take all his capital and leave him without anything in reserve if another killing blizzard nearly wiped him out. If he went to the bank for another loan, using the ranch as collateral, he would be putting himself back in the same position Maddie had just gotten him out of. He had no doubt he could make it, given that he would be able to reinvest all of the money in the ranch instead of paying it out to a grasping ex-wife, but he'd had enough of bank loans.

That left an investor. Robert Cannon was brilliant; he'd make one hell of a partner. And Reese did have a very clear business mind, so he could see all the advantages of a partnership. Not only would it broaden his financial base, he would be able to diversify, so the survival of the ranch wouldn't come down to a matter of how severe the winter was. The land was his own legacy to his child.

He picked up the telephone and punched the numbers on the card Robert had given him at Christmas.

When he put the receiver down half an hour later, it was all over except the paperwork. He and Robert dealt very well together, two astute men who were able to hammer out a satisfactory deal with a minimum of words. He felt strange, a little light-headed, and it took him a while to realize what had happened. He had voluntarily put his trust in someone else, surrendering his totalitarian control of the ranch; moreover, his new partner was a member of his wife's family, something he never could have imagined a year before. It was as if he had finally pulled free of the morass of hatred and resentment that had been dragging on him for years. April, finally, was in the past. He had made a mistake in his first choice of a wife; smart people learned from their mistakes and went on with their lives. He had learned, all right, but he hadn't gotten on with living until Maddie had taught him how. Even then he had clung to his bitter preconceptions until he had ruined his marriage.

God, he'd crawl on his hands and knees if it would convince her to come back.

As the days passed he slowly became desperate enough to do just that, but before the need inside him became uncontrollable, he received a phone call that knocked the wind out of him. The call was from April's sister, Erica. April was dead, and he was the main beneficiary in her will; would he please come?

Erica met him at JFK. She was a tall, lean, reserved woman, only two years older than April, but she had always seemed more like an aunt than a sister. Already there was a startling streak of gray in the dark hair waving back from her forehead, one she made no attempt to hide. She held out her hand to him in a cool, distant manner. "Thank you for coming, Reese. Given the circumstances, it's more than I expected and certainly more than we deserve."

He shrugged as he shook her hand. "A year ago I would have agreed with you."

"What's happened in the past year?" Her gaze was direct.

"I remarried. I got back on my feet financially."

Her eyes darkened. She had gray eyes, too, he noticed, though not that soft, slumberous dove gray of Maddie's eyes. "I'm sorry about what happened in the divorce. April was, too, after it was over, but there didn't seem to be any way to make amends. And I'm glad you remarried. I hope you're very happy with your wife."

He would be, he thought, if he could only get her to live with him, but he didn't say that to Erica. "Thank you. We're expecting a baby around the end of October."

"Congratulations." Her severe face lightened for a moment, and she actually smiled, but when the smile faded he saw the tiredness of her soul. She was grieving for her sister, and it couldn't have been easy for her to call him.

"What happened to April?" he asked. "Was she ill?"

"No, not unless you want to call it an illness of the spirit. She remarried, too, you know, less than a year after your divorce, but she was never happy and divorced him a couple of years ago.''

It was on the tip of his tongue to ask if she'd taken Number Two to the cleaners, too, but he bit it back. It would be petty of him in the face of Erica's grief. Once he would have said it, once he had been bitter enough that he wouldn't have cared who he wounded. Maddie had changed that.

"She had started drinking heavily," Erica continued. "We tried to convince her to get therapy, to control it, and for a while she tried to stop on her own. But she was sad, Reese, so sad. You could see it in her eyes. She was tired of living."

He drew in a sharp breath. "Suicide?"

"Not technically. Not intentionally. At least, I don't think so. I can't let myself think it was. But she couldn't stop drinking, because it was the only solace she had. The night she died, she'd been drinking heavily and was driving back from Cape Cod. She went to sleep, or at least they think that's what happened, and she became one more statistic on drunk driving.'' Erica's voice was calm and unemotional, but the pain was in her eyes. She reached out and awkwardly touched his arm, a woman who found it as difficult to receive comfort as she did to give it.

On the taxi ride into the city he asked, "Why did she make me her main beneficiary?"

"Guilt, I think. Maybe love. She was so wild about you in the beginning, and so bitter after the divorce. She was jealous of the ranch, you know. After the divorce, she told me she would rather you'd had a mistress than own that ranch, because she could fight another woman, but that chunk of ground had a hold on you that no woman could equal. That's why she went after the ranch in the divorce, to punish you." She gave him a wry smile. "God, how vindictive people can be. She couldn't see that she simply wasn't the type of wife you needed. You didn't like the same things, didn't want the same things out of life. When you didn't love her as much as you loved the ranch, she thought it was a flaw in her rather than accepting it as the difference between two very different people."

Reese had never thought of April in that light, never seen their marriage and subsequent divorce through her eyes. The only thing he had seen in her had been the bitterness, and that was what he had allowed to color his life. It was a blow to learn the color had been false, as if he had been wearing tinted lenses that had distorted everything.

He spent the night in a hotel, the sort of hotel he had once taken for granted. It felt strange to be back on firm financial ground again, and he wondered if he had ever truly missed the trappings of wealth. It was nice to be able to afford the posh minisuite, but he wouldn't have minded a plain motel. The years without money had rearranged his priorities.

The reading of the will the next day didn't take much time. April's family, too caught up in their grief to be hostile, was subdued. So was her father. April had thoroughly thought out the disposal of her possessions, as if she had anticipated her death. She divided her jewelry and personal possessions among family members, likewise the small fortune in stocks and bonds she had owned. It was her bequest to him that left him stunned.

"To Gideon Reese Duncan, my former husband, I leave the amount of his divorce settlement to me.

Should he precede me in death, the same amount shall be given to his heirs in a gesture of fairness too long delayed.''

The lawyer droned on, but Reese didn't hear any of it. He couldn't take it in. He was in shock. He leaned forward and braced his elbows on his knees, staring at the Oriental rug under his feet. She had given it all back, and in doing so had shown him the stark futility of the years of hatred.

The most ironic thing was that he had already let go of it. The inner darkness hadn't been able to withstand Maddie's determination. Even if he had never been able to rebuild the ranch to its former size, he would have been happy as long as he had Maddie. He had laughed with her and made love with her, and somewhere along the way his obsession had changed into a love so powerful that now he couldn't live without her, he could only exist.

His heart suddenly squeezed so painfully that he almost grabbed his chest. Hell! How could he have been so stupid?

Come home with me.

Give me one good reason why I should.

That was all she'd asked for, one good reason, but he hadn't given it to her. He'd thrown out reasons, all right, but not the one she'd been asking for, the one she needed. She'd all but told him what it was, but he'd been so caught up in what he needed that he hadn't paid any attention to what *she* needed. How simple it was, and now he knew what to say.

Give me one good reason why I should.

Because I love you.

* * *

He strode through the door of Floris's café and stood in the middle of the room. The increase in customers was still going strong, maybe because Floris was safely isolated in the kitchen and Maddie was out on the floor charming everyone with her lazy drawl and sexy walk.

As usual, silence fell when he entered and everyone turned to look at him. Maddie was behind the counter, wiping up a coffee spill while she exchanged some good-natured quips with Glenna Kinnaird. She looked up, saw him and went still, her eyes locked on him.

He hooked his thumbs in his belt and winked at her. "Riddle me this, sweetheart. What has two legs, a hard head and acts like a jackass?"

"That's easy," she scoffed. "Reese Duncan."

There was a muffled explosion of suppressed snickers all around them. He could see the amusement in her eyes and had to grin. "How are you feeling?" he asked, his voice dropping to a low, intimate tone that excluded everyone else in the café and made several women draw in their breath.

Her mouth quirked in that self-amusement that made him want to grab her to him. "This isn't one of my good days. The only thing holding me together is static cling."

"Come home with me, and I'll take care of you."

She looked him in the eye and said quietly, "Give me one good reason why I should."

Right there in front of God and most of Crook, Montana, he drew in a deep breath and took the gamble of a lifetime, his words plain and heard by all, because no one was making even the pretense of not listening.

"Because I love you."

Maddie blinked, and to his surprise he saw her eyes glitter with tears. Before he could start forward, however, her smile broke through like sunshine through a cloud bank. She didn't take the time to go around the counter; she climbed on top of it and slid off on the other side. "It's about time," she said as she went into his arms.

The customers broke into applause, and Floris came out of the kitchen. She sniffed and looked displeased when she saw Madelyn hanging in Reese's arms with her feet off the floor. "I suppose this means I've got to get another waitress," she muttered.

Someone muttered back, "Hell, Floris, if you'll just stay in the kitchen we'll find you another waitress."

"It's a deal," she said, and startled everyone in the café by actually smiling.

He didn't wait to get back to the house before he made love to her; as soon as they were on Duncan land he stopped the truck and pulled her astride him. Madelyn thought her heart would burst as she listened to his roughly muttered words of love and lust and need. She couldn't get enough of touching him; she wanted to sink into his skin, and she tried to.

When they finally got to the house he carried her inside and up the stairs to their bedroom, where he placed her on the big bed and began stripping her. She laughed, a drugged, wanton sound, as she stretched languidly. "Again?"

"I want to see you," he said, his voice strained. When she was naked he was silent, struck dumb and enchanted by the changes in her body. They were still slight, but obvious to him because he knew every inch of her. There was just beginning to be a faint curve to her belly, and her breasts were a little rounder, even firmer than before, her nipples darkened to a lush reddish brown. He leaned forward and circled one with his tongue, and her entire body quivered. "God, I love you," he said, and laid his head on her belly, his arms locked around her hips.

Madelyn slid her fingers into his hair. "It took you long enough," she said gently.

"What I lack in quickness, I make up in staying power."

"Meaning?"

"That I'll still be telling you that fifty years from now." He paused and turned his head to kiss her stomach. "I have something else to tell you."

"Is it good?"

"I think so. Things are going to be changing around here pretty soon."

"How?" She looked suspicious. "I'm not sure I want things to change."

"I have a new partner. I called Robert a week or so ago, and he bought in. We'll be expanding in a big way as soon as I can get started on it. This is now the Duncan and Cannon ranch."

Madelyn burst into laughter, startling him into lifting his head from her stomach. "Whatever you do," she said, "don't call it the D and C. I don't think I could live on a ranch named after a surgical procedure!"

He grinned, feeling everything in him come alive under the magic spell of her laughter. "It'll keep the same name," he said.

"Good." Slowly her laughter faded, and she gave him a somber look. "Why did you call him?"

"Because I trust you," he said simply. "Through you, I can trust him. Because it was a good business decision. Because I wanted to show you how a really good ranch operates. Because we're having a baby. Because, damn it, I'm too damn proud to be satisfied with a second-rate operation. Is that enough reasons?"

"The first one was good enough." She put her hands on his face and stared at him, her heart in his eyes. It rattled him, even while it made him feel as if he could conquer the world, to see how much Maddie loved him. He started to lean down to kiss her when she said seriously, "Did you know that a ten-gallon hat will really only hold about three quarts?"

On the third of November, Madelyn lay in a labor room in Billings, holding Reese's hand and trying to concentrate on her breathing. She had been there over twenty-four hours and she was exhausted, but the nurses kept telling her everything was fine. Reese was unshaven and had dark circles under his eyes. Robert was somewhere outside, wearing a rut in the tile of the hall.

"Give me another one," she said. Reese was looking desperate, but she needed something to get her mind off herself.

"India ink really comes from China."

"You're really scraping the bottom of the barrel, aren't you? Let's see." A contraction interrupted her, and she squeezed his hand as it surged and peaked, then fell off. When she could speak again she said, "The sounds of stomach growling are called borborygmus." She gave him a triumphant look.

He cradled her hand against his cheek. "You've been reading the dictionary again, and that's cheating. I've got a good one. The San Diego Chargers got their name because the original owner also owned the Carte Blanche credit card company. 'Charge' is what he wanted the cardholders to say."

She laughed, but the sound was abruptly cut off as another contraction seized her. This one was a little different in intensity, and in the way it made her feel. She panted her way through it, staring at the monitor with blurring eyes so she could see the mechanical confirmation of what she felt. She lay back against his arm and said weakly, "I don't think it's going to be much longer."

"Thank God." He didn't know if he could hold out much longer. Watching her in pain was the hardest thing he had ever done, and he was seriously considering limiting the number of their children to one. He kissed her sweaty temple. "I love you, sweetheart."

That earned him one of her slow smiles. "I love you, too." Another contraction.

The nurse checked her and smiled. "You're right, Mrs. Duncan, it won't be much longer. We'd better get you into delivery."

He was with her during delivery. The doctor had kept careful watch on the growing baby and didn't think she'd have any trouble delivering it. Reese wondered violently if the doctor's idea of trouble differed from his. It was thirty-six hours since her labor had begun. Less than half an hour after he'd told her about the San Diego Chargers, Reese was holding his red, squalling son in his hands.

Madelyn watched him through tear-blurred eyes, smiling giddily. The expression on Reese's face was so intense and tender and possessive that she could barely stand it. "Eight pounds, two ounces," he murmured to the infant. "You just barely made it under the wire."

Madelyn laughed and reached for both husband and son. Reese settled the baby in her arms and cradled her in his, unable to take his eyes from the both of them. He'd never seen anything so beautiful in his life, even if her hair was matted with sweat and coming loose from her braid. God, he felt good! Exhausted but good.

She yawned and rested her head against his shoulder. "I think we did a good job," she announced, examining the baby's tiny fingers and damp dark hair. "I also think I'm going to sleep for a week."

When she was in her room, just before she did go to sleep, she heard Reese say it again. "I love you, sweetheart." She was too sleepy to answer, but she reached out and felt him take her hand. Those were three words she never got tired of hearing, though she'd heard them often during the past months.

Reese sat and watched her as she slept, a smile in his eyes. Slowly his eyelids drooped as he succumbed to his weariness, but not once during his sleep did he turn loose of her hand.

What do you do if everything you ever
wanted is

Against the Rules

It had been years since Rule Jackson had last seen her.
Cathryn Ashe wanted desperately to forget the man who'd
claimed her heart and her innocence that sultry summer
day. But now she was back and he still wanted her. Cathryn
knew that some things were never meant to be, and
yet…the passion he stirred up inside her couldn't be
denied even if it meant breaking all the rules!

From award-winning author

Linda Howard

Available in January, at your favorite retail outlet.

MIRA The brightest star in women's fiction

MLH2

Take 3 of "The Best of the Best™" Novels FREE
Plus get a FREE surprise gift!

Special Limited-time Offer

Mail to The Best of the Best™

3010 Walden Avenue
P.O. Box 1867
Buffalo, N.Y. 14269-1867

YES! Please send me 3 free novels and my free surprise gift. Then send me 3 of "The Best of the Best™" novels each month. I'll receive the best books by the world's hottest romance authors. Bill me at the low price of $3.74 each plus 25¢ delivery and applicable sales tax, if any.* That's the complete price and a savings of over 10% off the cover prices—quite a bargain! I understand that accepting the books and gift places me under no obligation ever to buy any books. I can always return a shipment and cancel at any time. Even if I never buy another book from Harlequin, the 3 free books and the surprise gift are mine to keep forever.

183 BPA ANV9

Name	(PLEASE PRINT)	
Address		Apt. No.
City	State	Zip

This offer is limited to one order per household and not valid to current subscribers.
*Terms and prices are subject to change without notice. Sales tax applicable in N.Y. All orders subject to approval.

UBOB-295   ©1990 Harlequin Enterprises Limited

Bestselling Author

ERICA SPINDLER

Introduces you to the woman called

Red

Everybody loves Red—whoever she is. A haunted
teenager who defied the odds to find fame as a top model.
A pretty face who became a talented fashion photographer.
A woman who has won the love of two men. Yet, no
matter how often she transforms herself, the pain of Red's
past just won't go away—until she faces it head on....

Available this July, at your favorite retail outlet.

MIRA The brightest star in women's fiction   MESR

New York Times Bestselling Author

JAYNE ANN KRENTZ

Sometimes having too much money can be a curse.

Full Bloom

Emily Ravenscroft is a woman who doesn't need her
wealthy, overbearing family to tell her that money can't
buy love. Her problem is finding a man who can't be
bought. And Jacob Stone might just be that man—provided
Emily can survive the unwanted advances of a bitter
ex-fiancé....

Available this July at your favorite retail outlet.

 MIRA The brightest star in women's fiction   MJAKFB

If you are looking for more titles by

LINDA HOWARD

Don't miss these passionate stories by one of
MIRA's bestselling authors:

#66011	ALMOST FOREVER	$4.99 U.S.	☐
		$5.50 CAN.	☐
#66033	THE CUTTING EDGE	$4.99 U.S.	☐
		$5.50 CAN.	☐

(limited quantities available on certain titles)

TOTAL AMOUNT	$
POSTAGE & HANDLING	$
($1.00 for one book, 50¢ for each additional)	
APPLICABLE TAXES*	$_____
TOTAL PAYABLE	$_____
(check or money order—please do not send cash)	

To order, complete this form and send it, along with a check or money
order for the total above, payable to MIRA Books, to: **In the U.S.:**
3010 Walden Avenue, P.O. Box 9077, Buffalo, NY 14269-9077; **In Canada:**
P.O. Box 636, Fort Erie, Ontario, L2A 5X3.

Name:_____

Address:_____City:_____

State/Prov.:_____ Zip/Postal Code:_____

*New York residents remit applicable sales taxes.
 Canadian residents remit applicable GST and provincial taxes.   MLHBL3

MIRA